The Runaway

Other Lions titles you may enjoy

Joyce Stranger
Midnight Magic

Caroline Akrill
The Eventing Trilogy
Eventer's Dream
A Hoof in the Door
Ticket to Ride

Patricia Leitch
The Jinny series
1. For Love of a Horse
2. A Devil to Ride
3. The Summer Riders
4. Night of the Red Horse
5. Gallop to the Hills
6. Horse in a Million
7. The Magic Pony
8. Ride Like the Wind
9. Chestnut Gold
10. Jump for the Moon
11. Horse of Fire
12. Running Wild

Animal Sanctuary

③

The Runaway

Joyce Stranger

Lions
An Imprint of HarperCollinsPublishers

I owe thanks to Ann Cragg and Barbara Emptage of
the Glantraeth Animal Sanctuary, Anglesey,
for letting me share their weekends and "borrow"
their animals for my stories.
To Eileen Clark who rescued the real Blue,
and to Joe Naylor of the Brynterion working farm
for letting me watch a breach calving.
To David, Alison and Mark at the sea zoo
which I have watched grow.
To Les and Denise Edwards whose bitch Jess and
dog Nikos have given me the best pup I ever had.

*The stories in this trilogy are works of fiction; the
events are imaginary; the characters, farms and
villages bear no resemblance to any person or place.*

First published in the U.K. in 1992 in Lions

Lions is an imprint of HarperCollins Children's Books,
a division of HarperCollins Publishers Ltd,
77–85 Fulham Palace Road, Hammersmith,
London W6 8JB

Printed and bound in Great Britain by
HarperCollins Book Manufacturing Ltd, Glasgow

Chapter 1

There was a rip roaring swashbuckling throat catching gale that tore across the sea, hurling mountainous waves against the promenades to die in a whirl of spray. The wind screamed through the trees, flinging the branches high and then tossing them against a sky that spun with racing clouds.

Martin Slater, bent almost double, fighting his way up the hill, looked at the German Shepherd racing beside him. Blue's mouth was gaping, his eyes alight with fun, even though his fur stood on end and he had difficulty beating against the storm.

"Got to go to Caernarfon and pick up two sick seagulls and an owl with a broken wing," Dannie had said just after lunch. "No one is going to visit the Animal Park today. Coming? Bring Blue and take him for a walk. I'll pick up some food for the pigs as well."

Martin leaped at the chance. Life on the farm was a race from the time the morning alarm went off at 5 a.m. until he dropped into bed, too tired to think, around ten o'clock.

School days were a memory. I didn't know I was born, Martin thought. School was a rest cure compared with helping in the family business. A working farm open to the public needed all kinds of animals, not just a few. People wanted to see the cattle milked, to see the sheep and their lambs, to watch the shearing; they were fascinated by every detail of the procedure that, after almost six years, seemed so much a matter of course to him.

Time taken showing visitors around and explaining the working of the farm meant most evenings were spent finishing all the interrupted chores. Every creature needed food and water and a clean cage or enclosure.

Many needed much more than that.

It was difficult to remember when he was twelve and not only hated the farm but was terrified of the animals. He hated everything about his life then. He hated living in Wales. He loathed his stepfather and detested his two stepsisters.

He spent much of the first two years of his mother's new marriage planning to run away, and also planning revenge on his real father for deserting them when Martin was only five. He could laugh at his twelve-year-old self now. His own father had gone to Australia and it would be very difficult to find him again, as they had no address. But that desertion still had the power to hurt him.

He remembered crouching in his bedroom, afraid, as his parents yelled at one another, and often yelled at him. It had been a relief when his father left. Life had been good for the next seven years even if they hadn't had much money. Just the two of them. And then his mother re-married and suddenly there were five of them. Worst of all being English made him an outsider, at home and at school.

He'd felt a complete outcast until Blue came into his life; starving, abandoned, and unhappy. As unhappy as Martin himself.

Boy and dog had bonded instantly and Taid, his step grandfather, had helped him turn an unacceptable waif into a well-trained companion that everyone loved.

Martin watched the river rage below them, the water high with rain from the hills. Boulders rumbled and moaned as they were tumbled from their beds. Blue longed to dive in, but that would be dangerous. He held the lead tightly, scolding his dog gently for the sudden eager pull towards the water.

It was good to relax, even if the day was wild. The roaring wind was a background to his thoughts. Even though they were always so busy, the Sanctuary and the Animal Park were often fun and they were a major part of his life.

His skill with figures had helped him come to terms with his new family and now he and his stepfather were, if not friends, at least able to tolerate one another and sometimes find common ground.

Blue's sudden bark startled him as did the slim long shape of a wild animal that shot across the path, a young yellow Labrador in hot pursuit. Blue strained on the lead.

Martin thought the animal was a polecat but wasn't sure. He'd only caught a brief glimpse before it vanished into the undergrowth, the dog panting after it.

As the two disappeared, Blue's ears pricked forward, and he pawed impatiently at Martin's leg, his whole attitude saying "Look. Haven't you seen it?"

Martin's eyes followed the direction of the dog's pointing ears. They didn't need words to understand one another. Martin knew now by instinct what the dog wanted. His mind flashed back to those early days when Taid had helped him train the dog and also, though Martin didn't then realize it, helped him come to terms with his new life.

"Learn to read your dog, Bach," the old man said, time and time again. "He's telling you. Look at him."

In those early days Martin had looked and been baffled. Now it was hard to understand how clueless he had been. He could not only read his own dog, but other peoples' dogs too and know at once if the owners were kind or hard on them.

Taid, when he died a couple of years ago, left Martin and his stepsisters money in trust to start them in their adult lives. Martin still missed the old man. Time to return to the present.

He sighed.

There, on the ground, not twenty feet away from them, lay a tiny animal. He had thought it a dead mouse or rat that the polecat -- or whatever it was -- had been carrying in it's mouth. But whatever lay on the ground was moving.

"Blue, stay," he said, knowing his dog would obey, however much he longed to investigate. He walked across the tussocky grass and squatted down to inspect it. It was a baby polecat. Its eyes were still closed, and it squeaked its misery. It couldn't be more than a few days old. Martin put down a hand to it and it seized his finger, trying to suck.

That was the end of his longed for leisure. He would have to find Dannie and get it back to the farm fast, so that his stepsister, Anna Wyn, who was in charge of all the wild invalids, could feed it. Two hourly feeds day and night. More work and he wouldn't be popular, but how could he leave it to die? The dog might come back and kill it brutally, before the mother found it again. If she even came to look. If she hadn't been killed herself.

An out of breath woman came up to him.

"I've lost my dog. Have you seen a young Labrador? He ran off. I think the wind excited him."

Martin, thinking of the effort that would be involved in rearing the polecat kitten, and of the mother's misery, if she were even alive, lost his temper.

"Your dog has just been responsible for orphaning this." He held out the baby. "He may well have killed its mother. If you can't control him, keep him on a lead. The animals in the woods have as much right to life as he has. People like you shouldn't have dogs."

Her terrified expression made him feel guilty. A moment later he realized she was also afraid of him towering above her, furious with her, the two of them alone in a windy wood. Civilization was a mile or so away.

The thought of that mile spurred him to action.

"The dog went that way. Keep him on a lead if you can't get him to come when he's called and for goodness' sake take him to be educated at a decent dog class. Blue, come."

He held his breath. Would his own dog let him down? Blue was watching the waving grass, his eyes bright and too interested. But the dog was anxious to see what his master had found and raced to him, sitting and looking eagerly at the tiny animal. Martin held it for the dog to sniff. Blue was well used to their orphans.

"Time to run," he said. He was aware of the woman watching him and hoped she had seen how well-controlled his own dog was.

The wind was against them all the way. Martin, head down, was almost unable to breathe, as the wind tore into his face. He held the orphan tight, running down the hill towards the car park, praying that Dannie would be there. Blue pranced beside him, excited by the weather.

Dannie, who had found Martin when he fell over and injured himself while running away two years before, was soon to marry Anna Wyn. And her sister Dilys was also engaged to marry the new young vet at the practice where she worked as nurse.

Everything keeps changing, Martin thought. Dannie had been part of the farm now for over two years and the big man was the only real friend Martin had. He had sold his own home and moved into Taid's cottage. Martin couldn't help being jealous of the time that Dannie spent with Anna Wyn, longing for the days when they had gone off walking together in their spare time, or rambled on the hills, Blue beside them. Dannie made him laugh with outrageous stories as he remembered a childhood that was so adventurous it surely had to be invented.

Martin was in luck. Dannie, lugging a sack of pigfood, was sauntering towards the Land Rover. Martin called at him from a hundred yards away.

"Dannie!"

Martin's yell carried on the wind and the big man turned and came towards him.

"World about to end?" he asked.

"No. Look at this."

"A polecat kitten! Niffs a bit, doesn't he? Where did you find the poor little beast?"

"A dog chased his mother and she dropped him. She ran off. I only hope the dog didn't get her as there'll be other babies in the nest. She must have been heavy in milk because she couldn't run fast."

"She saved this one's life, didn't she? OK, let's get moving. I was going to treat you to coffee and a sticky bun, but we need to get home."

Martin grinned. He had once adored the iced buns his stepsisters called sticky buns but his tastes were more sophisticated now. That didn't prevent Dannie teasing him, though.

The tiny animal was warm against Martin's

hand. He tucked him against his jersey, underneath his anorak. It was totally relaxed, and seemed unbothered by this amazing change in its lifestyle. Its movements were re-assuringly strong. It pushed its nose against its long otterlike tail and slept.Blue curled himself down at the back of the Land Rover and went to sleep. Journeys bored him unless he could see out of the window.

"Time this blew itself out," Dannie said, negotiating the narrow roads.

"I bet there are about ten times as many roadworks as usual. How long do you think he can survive without being fed?"

"A day or so. He'll be OK. Puppy milk should do him and we've plenty of that. Anna Wyn bought more yesterday for the Jack Russell pup you found."

"Oh Gerontius," Martin said. "I'd forgotten the pup."The family was liable to come out with some very odd expressions. Gwyn was a dedicated chapel-goer, and insisted his daughters and stepson never used bad language. He never used it himself and nor had Taid, but both of them were very strong men for all of that. What Gwyn said, you did. Fast.

"You won't be popular." Dannie negotiated a tricky curve and hooted at a driver too eager to come out from the right. "What did Gwyn say when we went through the accounts?"

13

"'No more orphans. Learn to say no. We're not making ends meet. What we make by opening the Park to tourists in the summer doesn't cover feed and vet bills for all the animals in the winter.'"

Martin could recite it off by heart. It was becoming a litany. They joked about it, but knew that it was only too true.

"Anna Wyn will never learn to say no to anything in need of care and attention. In fact I sometimes think she's marrying me because she sees me as a waif and stray."

"Better than being married for your money," Martin said.

"Enough to feed me and put a bit towards the wedding . . . not even enough for a car. I don't know how we'd manage if Gwyn didn't share the Land Rover. And the pigfood's gone up."

They seemed to think of nothing but money.

"The Animal Park would do fine if it wasn't for all the invalids people keep bringing," Dannie said, tapping impatiently on the steering wheel as the green light they were approaching changed to red. His mind, as ever, was racing away. "I think the two seagulls have botulism. One may survive; I'll be surprised if the other does. And the owl's wing has to be set; that means a hefty vet bill."

"We ought to charge them to dump on us," Martin said. "We've had two more rabbits and a gerbil this week alone; and no money for food for them. And even a gerbil has an appetite."

"Our animals all have appetites like pigs," Dannie said, slipping back into gear. "I only hope Gwyn is in a good mood and it isn't one of his more defeatist days."

"'We'll all be bankrupt and then what will you all do? Not one of you seems to have an idea in your head beyond flooding this place with mouths to feed,'" Martin said, quoting his stepfather again.

"It's not really funny. Two farms have given up in the last year. Life's tough on farmers and nobody seems to understand." Dannie steered round the roundabout that led to Britannia Bridge. "Blow it. It's closed because of the gale."

"First time I've known it completely closed," Martin said, aware of the wind buffeting the Land Rover. Dannie drove round the roundabout again and back on to the road leading to the old suspension bridge.

Behind him, one of the seagulls was moving in the cardboard box that sheltered it. Blue, waking, nosed the box in curiosity.

"Leave it, Blue." Martin knew every move the dog made and was ready to check him when necessary.

"You could always become a police dog-handler if you don't make it any other way and we have to fold," Dannie said.

Martin laughed. "Remember what Taid used to say? Never give up while there's breath in your body and a farthing in the bank."

"Grand old man, Taid was. I remember him with the dogs at the Trials. He had a way with a dog that a lot of shepherds used to envy. That black collie of his, Tan . . . he was a dream, they say. Won everything going." Dannie turned on to the A4080 by the tollhouse and Martin sighed with relief. Only a few miles now and they would be home and the polecat kitten could be fed.

The Land Rover engine faltered, and stopped.

"Now what?" Dannie asked, as he clambered out. "You'll have to steer while I push her in to the side. Lucky it's wide here with the turning into Plas Newydd."

"Gwyn had her out yesterday. Did you look at the petrol gauge?"

Dannie switched on the engine and they looked at the telltale mark together.

"Where on earth did Gwyn go? I filled it the day before yesterday."

"Doesn't matter much," Martin said. "One of us has to walk back to Tyn Lon garage and get a can. Toss for it."

Dannie tossed a 2p coin.

"Heads," said Martin and grinned smugly as Dannie showed him the result.

"Have a good walk," he said. But after Dannie had gone, he settled down to worry. Suppose the

16

polecat kitten needed food so badly that he died before they got home? He didn't want it to die on him. He held the little animal and felt its small body breathing gently under his hand.

Life was too difficult. He had no doubt whatever that when Gwyn saw what he had brought home, his stepfather would explode with anger.

Once Gwyn had been placid but worry about the farm had made him short-tempered and his rages were becoming more frequent.

If only they could make more money for the animals. But how?

Chapter 2

The farm shop appeared to have been attacked by lunatics, two policemen were talking to Leah, and Anna Wyn sat, white-faced, with tearmarks down her cheeks, holding a tiny puppy that appeared very near to death.

"What on earth?" Dannie asked.

Martin, looking around, saw twelve-year-old Tag crouched against one of the windowseats, looking as if he wished the earth would open and swallow him up.

Tag Pritchard haunted the farm, coming there in every spare moment. He lived with his family in an enormous caravan about half a mile away.

The caravan, which Tag's family called a trailer, was in the field behind the nursery where Laura lived with her parents and brother Mike and cousin Jennet, whose own mother and father had died in a car crash when she was two.

Tag was always eager to help.

Everyone wished he wouldn't as he only had to move to create disaster. If there was a bucket of water he stumbled and overturned it. If he could leave a gate or door open he did. Tag tried his best, but only succeeded in making life even more difficult for everyone else.

But surely Tag couldn't have created the mess in the shop?

"Tag had a puncture," Leah, Martin's mother, said. She handed round sandwiches and poured coffee. At least the tables and chairs were undamaged though they had been overturned. It looked as if a whirlwind had swept through the place.

"That did this?"

"Three young men gave him a lift. He told them where he was going. They paid and walked round, and then one of them came in to say that a pony had jumped the fence and hurt itself."

"So Anna Wyn went to look and so did I," Tag said. "All the ponies were out and the pigs and the goats and you know how Maggie hates other animals. She was kicking and bucking and chivvying everything."

"They'd hit her and scared her," Tag said. "She's a great slash across her back from a stick."

"And then?"

"They had all the time in the world," the younger policeman said grimly. "They took the money from the till and the wishing well; all the chocolates and the ice cream have gone, and many of the toys. Unfortunately Tag didn't notice the number of the car, and nor did any one else. An old blue Ford, and how many of those are there?"

"I didn't bank this week," Anna Wyn said. "I thought the till was safe. After all it's well hidden under the shelf, and it ought to have sounded an alarm. Only it didn't."

"They had all the time in the world," Leah repeated forlornly, looking at the room with only two thoughts in her head: that it would take hours to clean up, and would the insurance pay for the stolen money? They didn't even know exactly how much was in the till, as they hadn't totalled for the last two days.

"At least they haven't harmed any other animal; and they didn't go into the farmhouse," Leah said. "That was empty too."

It did not seem the right time to introduce the little polecat. Martin walked out of the farm shop and went to the little shed that served as hospital. He picked up an empty cat carrying cage, and crossed the big yard to the farm, taking care not to be seen.

A little cardboard box, a small piece of blanket

and the polecat kitten was safe. Blue watched in amazement, as Dannie took the cage up to his bedroom. The puppy milk powder was kept in the kitchen.

Martin made up enough for one feed, and cooled it down, plunging the cow syringe that they used as feeder into cold water. The little creature sucked hungrily. It, at least, appeared to be very strong. He massaged its tummy with paper tissues until it emptied itself, and watched as it settled to sleep. He put the cage on his chest of drawers, away from the window and out of the draught. No one ever came into his bedroom without his permission, so the polecat wouldn't be found. Later, he would take his mother into his confidence.

Two-hourly feeds would be a big commitment, but Dannie and Leah would help, he was sure. Better not let Gwyn know about the polecat baby. And what was Gywn going to say about the robbery and vandalism?

He gave a last glance at the sleeping kitten. It was a very pretty creature, with smoky-coloured fur, a little otter-like head, and a long otter-like tail. More like an otter than anything else, Martin decided.

"Just like you to slope off and leave all the work to us", Anna Wyn flared at him as Martin returned to the shop.

"I gave Martin an errand," Dannie said.

The two policemen had gone. Leah was picking up chairs and checking the counter.

"They even helped themselves to sandwiches and my homemade cakes," she said. "I just can't believe it. All the jams and chutneys have gone. They worked fast and were well organized."

"They paid to come in, and took that money as well," Anna Wyn said, as if it were the final indignity.

"Where did the pup come from?" Martin asked, trying to distract her. Not much use doing anything but try and clear up. Damage limitation, as Dannie called it when they had to rectify Tag's mistakes. Though this was far worse.

Tag had gone outside, and came running in.

"Both cockatiels and the two grey parrots have gone."

"The aviaries are padlocked."

"They cut the wire," Tag said. "There's holes beside the gate."

There was a screech of tyres as the police car came back into the yard.

Evan Price, who was new to the area, got out, and called them over.

"These yours?" he asked.

Four pairs of eyes looked at them from a box on the back seat. Two grey parrots and two cockatiels.

"We've got everything back," Evan said. "They were driving too fast, came round a blind bend and crashed into Joe's tractor which was travelling slowly on their side of the road. We found another team dealing with that crash when we came along. You'll get your money back in due course; doubt if you'll want the food or ice cream or chocolate. They made a right mess of the car and themselves."

He looked at them and grinned. "We're supposed to keep everything as evidence, but I doubt if we can cope with the birds, so they are released into your care. OK?"

"Are they badly hurt?" Leah asked.

"They'll survive to pay for what they did. And suffer for a week or so. 'Take what you want and pay for it,' says God. And people usually do, you know."

"The aviary needs repairing," Anna Wyn said. "And there's this puppy . . . it's a Rottweiler. Someone just threw it away. There were five others. They're all dead."

She looked down at the pup. It lay very still in her arms, but its eyes were open and fixed on hers.

"I don't know if it will survive either, poor little beast. I hate people."

Martin thought of the Rottweiler bitch at the hotel at Red Wharf Bay. They always went to see Sheba if they were in the area, and had time to stop for a sandwich and a drink. She was one of the gentlest dogs he knew.

"All the water bowls have been spilled during the afternoon's stampede," Dannie said. "Come on, Martin. No peace for the wicked."

"Eat first," Leah said. "There won't be any supper tonight. Gwyn went to market, and he won't be back till late, and Dilys isn't due in this evening. So we'll all have to turn to. I doubt if we'll be finished before midnight. I must clean this up and make more food for tomorrow. There's a good weather forecast."

The escapes had caused chaos. There were fences to mend, and the aviary to repair.

"Better put all the animals into the stables tonight. The goats are OK in their hut. The pigs aren't safe. They can go into the empty pigpens at the end of the farmyard. Good job Gwyn took that lot to market."

The Sanctuary was in a field of its own, away from the farm., Moving the animals took more time than even Martin had expected.

They worked on wearily, cursing the intruders.

"I hope they're all lame for life," Martin said uncharitably, as he walked across the park for the hundredth time, carrying wood to block a gap in the pheasant pen.

"They had a right royal time. Mindless idiots," Dannie said. "If I'd been here . . . "

"If we'd been here it probably wouldn't have happened." Martin eased his aching shoulders.

"I wonder if they'd have come here if they

hadn't given Tag a lift," Dannie said. Tag, finding himself unwelcome, had gone home.

"Not sure we can really blame him," Martin said.

"I spend half my time when he's here in cleaning up after him," Dannie said. "But one of his silly games with water gave me an idea." He yawned. "Am I tired!"

He sighed, and bit into his sandwich. They had both filled their pockets and were eating as they worked. No time to stop. No time to breathe. No time to think. School had been a picnic compared with this, Martin thought, as he filled two buckets with water. His arms ached and he had a blister on his right hand, just where the handle fitted. Only a few months ago, he hadn't known he was born.

The young Vietnamese Pot-Bellied Pigs began to grunt in unison.

"I don't believe it," Dannie said. "I bet none of the animals has been fed."

It was after 1 a.m when they finished the endless chores. Martin slipped away three times to feed the baby polecat. He would have to set his alarm to ring every two hours. He'd have to feed it that frequently or it would die.

Dannie came into the farm kitchen for a drink before going off to his own cottage and his bed.

"I never realized till tonight how many hours we spend taking water to the fields. I'm going to

25

find a pump. The animals can produce their own water. There are enough springs round the farm as well as the new lakes. It might save on our bills too as we won't be using the metered water."

"How do animals operate pumps?" Martin asked, bewildered. He was so tired that it was an effort even to think.

"With their noses. They soon learn. Especially if they're thirsty."

It was a good idea, and the next day Dannie went off to find a pump and install it in the top field, as an experiment.

They borrowed three men from the next-door farm and connected it up.

The only trouble was that the animals hadn't been consulted.

Chapter 3

Water seemed to have gone to Dannie's head.

He ran a series of pipes into every sty, each one ending, not in a tap, but in a push button, sited above an old stone trough.

"If the pigs don't learn to use them at least we can fill the bowls without carrying water," Dannie said.

Pigs, being pigs, soon found out that if they butted their noses or heads against the buttons, a fascinating gush of water appeared.

"Ferdie makes more work than the taps save," Anna Wyn complained. On sunny days, the young pig stood beneath the stream of water, his head pushing hard against the button, his eyes closed in ecstacy. This resulted in a remarkably soggy floor that had to be cleaned up.

"But look how popular he is. There are always people around his pen, watching him, and they tell others. He's responsible for half our clients."

Ferdie became even more popular when Tag threw him a football. Martin, about to tell the boy off, watched in disbelief as Ferdie tossed it with his head and caught it on his snout. He pushed it around the pen, delighting in its movement.

His cleverness brought him a much bigger enclosure, where he could flood the ground to his total content, and play with his ball whenever the mood seized him, which was often.

Tag, on holiday from school, played with him over the fence, throwing the ball for Ferdie to butt back. A local reporter, bringing his small son to the sanctuary one weekend, watched the performance. Ferdie became a star, with his picture on the front page of the local paper. Ferdie the Footballing Pig.

The first pump in the fields looked more like a boot cleaner than anything else. Martin watched as Dannie operated it with his foot and water fed into the container. Water, and nobody had to spend time carrying it. They would save hours every day.

Excitedly, Dannie and Martin, with Blue's help, herded twenty bullocks into the field. The bullocks, being curious, investigated the pump. Dannie worked the pump to show the bullocks.

"That's another good idea gone West," Dannie said in disgust as twenty bullocks bucked and bolted, terrified beyond reason. They had never seen water behave like that before.

They huddled, eyes white with fright, in the far corner of the field. They refused to graze and they refused to settle.

By teatime, Dannie gave up. The bullocks were herded back into a safer pasture where no strange object spurted at them.

"I don't know if it's a good thing or a bad thing that Gwyn's away," Dannie said. "At least we don't have to tell him of our failure."

"Or about the polecat and the new puppy," Martin said. "All the same, I wish he hadn't gone. There's so much to do."

"We're not that busy." Dannie was consoling. "You don't often get the chance of buying miniature ponies. They cost a fortune."

"Suppose the old lady doesn't like the idea of having them on show here?"

"Then we won't get them and there won't be so much work. Come on, Martin. What's the matter with you?"

I'm dog tired, Martin thought, but didn't say it. He was not going to admit that his stepsister managed two hourly feeds day and night without appearing any the worse for it while he was almost asleep on his feet.

The baby polecat was thriving and Martin was

surprised to find that he was fiercely protective. It was his find and his responsibility and he desperately wanted it to survive. So many baby animals died on them in the first few days. Now he knew how his stepsister felt about her charges.

"Might as well put Mrs P in the field that the bullocks hate," Dannie said. "Nothing ever upsets her."

Mrs Pilkington was a large Friesian cow who was placid until someone tried to milk her, when she outdid any bucking horse. She loathed the authomatic milker and kicked anyone trying to milk her by hand.

She was about to be sent away to justify her existence elsewhere when an ailing calf began to suckle her. Mrs Pilkington licked the baby's head, and from that moment the newcomer began to thrive.

She ambled happily up to the field behind Dannie, with her adopted calf in tow. She was a curious animal, investigating anything that was new.

"Oh, glory," Dannie said, as the cow stared about her and then marched determinedly over to the new pump. She nosed it. The bar gave way. She nosed it again, and was rewarded by a gush of water. Enthralled, she tried again, this time too gently. The water had come before and she had even tasted it. Why didn't it come now? She thrust her nose hard against the pedal, and water sprayed in a bright stream.

Delighted, she discovered that if she moved her head fast and only tipped the bar, more water came than before. Within minutes the container was full. She gulped thirstily and then called the calf to drink .

Dannie and Martin watched as she operated the pedal. She had learned in a few minutes to make it work far faster than Dannie had with his foot.

"The bullocks are never scared when Mrs P is there," Dannie said.

"So we put them back in the field tomorrow." Martin had no intention of moving bullocks that evening.

There was a shadow at the edge of the field. Martin and Dannie turned as Jennet came towards them. Jennet was as unlike her two cousins, Laura and Mike, as she could be with her neat cap of black hair and amazing dark eyes. She had been adopted when she was two years old after both her parents were killed in a motorway pile up.

"I came looking for sympathy," she said. "I won't get it from Laura and the girls. They're deep in wedding mania. I'll be glad when it's over. Laura's never designed a wedding dress before, and she's going all gooey about it. I'm not going to get married."

Dannie laughed.

"Maybe no one will ask you."

Jennet grinned. Martin had forgotten that any conversation with Jennet was liable at times to lead into a morass.

"I need help . . . and comforting with apples."

"Talk sense, love," Dannie said. "We're simple men and we're bone tired."

"If I talk sense I'll howl." Jennet was a few months younger than Martin. "Uncle has to cut back on expenses, owing to everything doing so badly, and he's had to sell Miracle. We were entered in most of the events this summer and did so well . . . but we just can't afford to keep him."

Everyone knew that Jennet adored the big bay. She had owned him for five years and won many local show-jumping competitions on him.

Dannie put an arm round her.

"Don't." Jennet pulled away from him. "Tell me not to be so stupid, or you'll have a wailing banshee on your hands."

"OK. Don't be stupid," Dannie said.

Jennet looked at him and then put out her tongue.

"You asked me." Dannie grinned at her, glad that she had relaxed.

"So what are you going to do?" Martin asked.

"Come and work with you. I'll come for nothing. I can take children pony trekking a couple of days each week. I can pay you a percentage of what I take. Please say yes. Life's such hell!" Tears threatened again.

"You needn't pay us anything," Dannie said. "We'll have to ask the others as we're all partners. But if you help with the Animal Park the days you aren't trekking then we'll count it as earned. Where are you going to take them?"

"My friend Sally has six horses, and lets them out. She's over on the mainland though and we'd need to drive the children there. She has seventeen acres of land, and has made a bridle trail all round it; it's absolutely safe."

"Insurance before we start. That'll cut into your profits. What will Sally charge you? "

"Nothing. That's the point. She got Miracle cheap. Very cheap. Uncle said that just to be rid of his keep and shoeing and vet bills would help enormously. I can ride him whenever I want and use the other ponies until I have a fund behind me. Then we go into it on a business basis. I might go into partnership with her later."

"Sounds as if you've found a whole new way of life. What are you moaning about? You haven't lost your horse for ever."

"But I don't have him to ride every day; or to school for jumping. I'll have to pay Sally if I ride him a lot; he isn't mine any more." She looked at them, desperate.

"Don't you see? I only just thought of half of it. You've cheered me up no end. Can I start tomorrow? I've left school too. No use making me go to college. I haven't as many brains as Mrs Pilkington."

"Have you told your family? Or Mike? Or Laura? What will they say? It's not much of a job." Martin looked at her anxiously, wondering how she got on with her cousins and their parents.

"Uncle says OK as long as I enjoy what I do. Auntie is super and all in favour."

Martin wished Jennet didn't always make him feel awkward. He ignored most girls and didn't much care what they thought of him, but for some reason he couldn't identify he wanted her to have a good opinion of him. He always ended up behaving like a clown.

She made him feel nine miles high and all fingers and thumbs.

"I was going to make the British Team, one day," Jennet said. "Oh well."

Laura's voice sounded behind her. "Want a lift home?"

Jennet looked at the sheaf of papers in her cousin's hand. Laura was slim and fair, her long hair lying on her shoulders. Blue eyes glinted in the last light of day.

"I'll walk," Jennet said, and turned off down the farm track.

"It's tough." Laura watched her cousin go. "She's a brilliant rider, and her horse deserves his name. But there's no way we can keep Miracle.

34

Dad had a family session; we all have to muck in and economize, or he'll have to sell up. That wouldn't help any of us."

"We know the feeling. How're the plans going for the dresses?" Laura had offered to design and make the bride's and bridesmaids' dresses for Martin's two step sisters.

"They should look gorgeous. We're making them ourselves."

She drove off, waving to her cousin as she passed. Jennet didn't see her. Her head was down, and she was walking slowly. Martin watched her, anxious. He was used to Jennet running everywhere, her eyes full of laughter.

"Hit her hard." Dannie yawned. "I'm whacked, and the leg that isn't mine is rubbing." He had lost a leg in the Falklands War. He was thankful that he had been able to move into Taid's old cottage on the farm. It made his life so much easier.

"Better look in on Merry," Martin felt responsible with his stepfather away. "She's due to calve any day now." If anything went wrong . . . it was the first time that Gwyn had ever left them on their own.

Dannie switched on the light in the stall where the young Friesian stood. She was restless and shaking her head, occasionally turning to eye her rear end as if it didn't belong to her, and what she saw bothered her.

"Hey, look at that!"

Dannie caught a note of panic in Martin's voice and came to join him. They stood together, staring at the two tiny white hooves that protruded from under Merry's tail.

"That calf's the wrong way round. Come on, Martin. It would happen when the gaffer's away. Not much sleep for either of us tonight. We'll have to help her ourselves. I only hope I know how Gwyn uses that calving tool."

Martin, turning away to find hot water, and the necessary equipment, wondered miserably if they would bring out a live calf. Neither of them had any experience of a breech birth, and they couldn't afford to call the vet.

"We can do it, Martin, " Dannie's voice said behind him. "Get a move on. She's been struggling for some time."

The yard was dark. Blue joined him, looking up as if the dog sensed his master's unease.

"In your bed, old boy. No walk tonight."

The dog lay down in the corner, sighing deeply. He stretched out and began to lick his paw thoughtfully. The Jack Russell pup that Martin had rescued was asleep in its box. Blue lifted it and carried it over to his own bed. It whimpered, pushed against him, and then settled.

Martin forgot them. He needed hot water, and there was no time to lose.

He glanced at the clock and nearly yelled aloud in exasperation. Time for the polecat baby's feed. He called to his mother as he filled the bucket.

"What's the problem?" She spoke from the top of the stairs, more than half asleep.

"Merry's calf's the wrong way round. And the polecat needs feeding. Dannie can't cope on his own."

He didn't see his mother's half smile as she came down the stairs to make up the milk for the little animal.

He raced back to the byre with the water, feeling desperate. Why did everything have to go wrong when his stepfather was away? He would never forgive himself if he lost the calf through his own inexperience.

The second thought hit him as he ran through the door. Suppose both cow and calf died? What would his stepfather say then?

Chapter 4

"She can't move the calf," Dannie said, as Martin returned. "She's not making the slightest effort. All her contractions seem to have stopped. I'd hoped she'd do it on her own."

He looked at the object Martin was holding. Martin always thought it was more like something invented by a crazy cartoonist than a very useful aid to any single-handed farmer. It resembled, more than anything, a giant screw, about five feet long, and several inches in diameter, with a bumper on the end and a cross bar half way to which was attached a lever.

"You'd better use it. You've seen Gwyn in action. I haven't. " He looked thoughtfully at the cow, who was watching them with an anxious expression on her face, and eyes that were desperately worried. "We're taking a risk."

Martin stared at him, wishing he hadn't voiced his opinion. If they failed they would have to confess to Gwyn that they had botched the job and produced a dead cow and a dead baby. And a loss for the farm in more ways than one. Merry bred good calves. This was her third, although they had only owned her a short time.

Gwyn had chosen her with care.

They had no choice. There was no other way to produce the calf.

Martin felt as if he had no experience at all. He had managed many an emergency, but never one like this. He swallowed. It had to be done.

"I've watched Gwyn. I know how to connect it. We tie the ropes round the calf's hooves, and attach the loops to the hooks on the cross bar. It looks so easy when he does it."

"We're going to find out the hard way whether it's easy or not." Martin was very glad that Dannie was there. Even if he did, uncharacteristically, seem less optimistic than usual.

There was a sudden mew from above them. Pirate, Ginger's kitten, now a massive cat, was sitting on one of the rafters, staring down into the straw below him with enormous interest.

"All we need now is a rat," Dannie said, disgust in his voice. "If Pirate starts to chase it, it'll upset the cow. We need some quiet here, and you need to concentrate." He walked over to the straw pile, to try and see what the cat was watching. Martin tied the calving ropes round the two tiny hooves. They seemed motionless and he prayed that the calf wasn't dead.

Dannie made a dive into the straw.

"Tag! Do you know what time it is?"

"Of course I know. Can I watch?"

"You can get off home. Your parents will be worrying about you." Dannie's voice was unusually impatient, and Tag reacted fast and angrily.

"They won't. They don't care what I do. Anyway I climbed out of the window and they don't know I'm out. I'm never going home. I hate my father. He's a big bully and he's never fair."

"We've a cow in trouble, Tag. We haven't time for you too. Out, and go home." Dannie took Tag by the collar and marched him into the darkness. He closed the door.

"I hate you too." The yell came to them across the yard.

"Of all the days to choose. I wonder what that was all about?"

Dannie stood by as Martin carefully pressed the buffer against the cow and began to work the lever. It was far more difficult that he had thought.

He gritted his teeth and prayed. It looked so simple when Gwyn did it.

Suppose he moved the lever too fast, dragged the calf out too fast, injured the cow as he did so? He wished his stepfather were there, at least to supervise. He had never realized how much skill was needed in even the simplest job around the farm, until he left school. This one was far from simple. Nor was it anything like the scenes in the TV series on farming vets. That was more than thirty years out of date, back in the dark ages, with anti-biotics only just beginning to be used. The modern farmer was a technician, and, if he were to survive, had to have more skills than in the old days. Martin wished, more than ever, that he had taken more notice. They had only needed to use the tool twice during the past year. Most calves came without difficulty.

Slowly, firmly, gently. He concentrated. Steady, steady, careful not to jerk. He held his breath. Please God, let me do it right. How much was Merry worth? Some hundreds of pounds and so would the calf be in due course. He hoped it was female; they needed more for breeding. He had never before appreciated that though his stepfather made a muddle of anything financial, he was a brilliant stockman.

His animals all loved him, even the cows and the little bull calf, coming to greet him when he went into their field. He would be upset to find he had been wrong about Merry's calving date. He would never have gone away had he thought she was due. Martin resented what he thought was a lack of trust, but now he realized that it was not that at all.

It was a desire to ensure that every animal on the farm had the best attention possible when needed. And the knowledge that neither Martin nor Dannie were, as yet, experienced enough. No amount of book learning could make up for years of working with animals. There was something new to learn every day.

Martin continued to pull, steadily, but gently. Suddenly there was a slithering sound and the rest of the calf appeared. Dannie caught the little calf as it began to fall. A heifer. She lay on the straw, lifeless.

"Now what do we do?"

What did Gwyn do? Martin took the two front legs and began to move them. He thumped the tiny chest. He took a piece of straw and tickled the calf's nostrils. She sneezed, and then drew in air with a tremendous heave.

"That's it. That's what Gwyn watches for. That first suck of air. Look, she's breathing now. She's O.K."

The calf moved her head and stared at them and Martin felt a sudden thrill of excitement. He had an absurd desire to dance and shout with joy. He had done that. He had helped the cow give birth. He had made the baby breathe. It was alive, it was moving, it was shaking an ear, it was staring at him out of puzzled eyes as if trying to make sense of this world into which it had been precipitated. It was his first baby, all his own work, without anyone standing behind him to tell him what to do.

He felt ten feet tall and was aware that he was grinning absurdly, as if his muscles had no control over his mouth.

Dannie swiftly dabbed the remains of the cord with antiseptic, ensuring that no germs could enter and cause problems later.

"You did it." He sounded jubilant. "Great. I'll take Merry and milk her," he added, knowing that Gwyn always drew off the first milk to give to the calf, to make sure it had had enough. That precious fluid contained colostrum, without which the baby would have no immunity to any illness. "The colostrum will be gone in a few hours and she doesn't look as if she's in the best of health herself."

"Not surprised, after all that. I reckon she needs a calcium drip," Martin said. "I'd better find it and set it up." That at least he had done before, as Gwyn treated his cows after birth with a drip as a matter of course. No harm if not necessary and it saved immense problems if it were.

When Martin had connected it up, Dannie held the bottle in the air, while the fluid fed into Merry's veins, through the needle pushed under her skin. It didn't seem to bother her. She stood patiently while the milk was sucked from her.

Merry was used to the machines. She stood, and Martin watched the drip anxiously, praying he had made no mistakes in setting it up. The scene reminded him of TV serials where nurses charged along beside trolleys on which their patients lay, while the bottles were held in the air, keeping the tubes unkinked as they raced to the operating theatre.

Martin tried hard to remember every detail of the procedure after calving. Taid always gave the cows a drink of gruel with what he called Farmer's Magic in it. Gwyn did not, but Martin was determined to have Merry as fit as was possible. She had had a bad time.

He mixed the feed in a bucket. Taid's potion was on a shelf. He wondered whether to use it, but the mixture was two years old and he didn't know what was in it. Ought to be thrown away. He added a huge dollop of treacle, which all the cows adored.

It was nearly three in the morning before they had finished. The afterbirth was slow to come away. Martin didn't want to leave her until he was sure that there was no undue bleeding.

Dannie made coffee and sandwiches. They took it in turns to wash and then sat on the straw bales, while Pirate pawed at their knees, begging for crumbs.

Martin, watching, was worried. Merry seemed to have no interest in the calf.

"Needs another of Taid's tricks," he said, astounded at how much he remembered of the old man's teaching. It was nearly two years since his step-grandfather had died, but he remembered him as if it were yesterday. He went into the kitchen and returned with the salt cellar.

He sprinkled salt lavishly along the calf's back and helped her to her fee. She stared up at her mother. Merry, as if half-remembering what she should do, licked tentatively along the baby's spine.

She tasted the salt, and, suddenly eager, began to lick in earnest. Within minutes, she had nosed the calf and recognized it as hers. Her tongue swept out, this time because she wanted to lick, and not because of the taste of salt.

"She'll do," Dannie said. "Pity we have to take it from her so soon. It's one for Mrs P. Merry's needed for the milking herd. Funny how they don't mind losing the calf after a few hours, but create no end if you leave it with them for two days. I suppose it takes time for the bond to form."

Bed called him. But as he entered the room, a small head lifted and whimpered excitedly. he had completely forgotten the little polecat and it was time for his feed. Wearily, he dragged imself downstairs, trying to keep his eyes open.

He mixed the feed and went up again to sit on the edge of his bed, holding the tiny animal as it fed.

Dear Heaven, he was tired, yet even when he fell into bed, he was unable to sleep, and wondered how they knew that the cows didn't mind losing their calves within hours of giving birth. The excitement of seeing the new life come still mastered him. What had Taid said? He'd never understood till now.

"It's always a miracle. Two beasts where there was one before, and the mothers nearly always so proud of them. I never tire of it. I wouldn't change places with anyone in the world when it comes to a birth on the farm."

Me too, Martin thought. He revelled in the unusual feeling of utter satisfaction, though he preferred sheep farming to cattle rearing. The lambs were left with their mothers much longer. On the other hand, when they were taken away, there was a bawling that seemed to go on for days.

Just before falling asleep he remembered Tag's sudden yell. The boy would be home by now, and fast asleep. Momentarily, he was worried. Tag was often dramatic, but never quite as bad as he had been that night. He was becoming a bit of a problem. Not his problem, Martin thought, just before he fell asleep.

It seemed no time at all before the alarm

shrilled at five o' clock for early milking. At least he had Dannie to help him while Gwyn was away.

Martin dragged on jeans, thick shirt, and anorak and boots, flapped cold water over his face, and went downstairs. Shaving and washing came after the cattle were in the field again, not before.

Before he could start milking he would have to feed the polecat, too. Anna Wyn, almost speechless with sleep, had mixed extra feed when she prepared it for her puppy and he took the syringe gratefully, having saved precious time.

His mother appeared just as he took the polecat from its cage.

"I'll take over. You get on, or we'll never get through the day."

He raced downstairs again. Anna Wyn always left coffee percolating in the pot that stood there all day, over a spirit lamp. Probably lethal, but the caffeine gave him a needed kick, Martin thought, as he poured himself a mug.

He whistled to Blue, whose small charge whimpered as his warm companion left him, and they went out into the yard. Blue, used to the routine, followed Martin to the field gate, and expertly herded the cows as they came out into the lane. No early drivers to make life difficult at this time, and with luck they'd be back again before anyone was up.

By the time the herd was assembled in the yard Dannie had the first group in the stalls and had fixed the cups. Martin, without thinking, checked the sound and suck of the pump. There were days when it stuttered and faltered, but today it was going well.

He looked in on Merry, who delighted him by eating as if she had been starved for days. The calf, now standing and moving with more confidence, was obviously full of life. Martin watched them for a while. You never forget the first time for anything, Taid used to say. People might die, but their memory stayed and the things they taught you were never forgotten.

As he led the cattle back to the field Martin realized that his life had changed again, overnight. It seemed to change all the time, as if he were being moulded into a different person. Somewhere, there was an understanding of the way life worked, but it was a ghost thought, a teasing memory.

Soon he would be eighteen. Old enough to vote. Old enough to go to the local with Gwyn and Dannie and have a drink if he wanted it.

Taid had left him income from a trust when he was eighteen. He had thought he'd go to college and be a vet. Now he wasn't sure. All those years before he was out in the real world.

One of the cows had slipped out of the herd and was trotting up the lane. Blue detached himself from Martin's side and turned her, herding her back to the rest.

They'd both learned so much, but there was so much more to learn. Martin closed the gate. No more time for deep thoughts. The day's panic was due to begin as soon as he had eaten breakfast. A bright sun meant the visitors would soon be coming. They opened at ten.

Without Gwyn, he'd have to take the visitors round the farm trail and explain how everything worked. He had never done that before either. Gwyn ought not to have gone away, but the miniature ponies they'd heard about were in the South of England, and the farmer had decided to look round and see if he could bring any other unusual animals back for Anna Wyn.

The Animal Park was beginning to be a big attraction. It had earned its keep and more, the year before. People came back again. All the same, it was slavery. Other people had holidays. None of them had ever had a holiday. Which was probably why Gwyn had prolonged his visit South, delighted to have a few days away from the farm. Animals had to be fed and cleaned out every day of the year; they didn't know about weekends or time off.

Martin connected the hose and began to swill down the yard. Blue retreated indoors to take up his proxy parental duty again, and watch the puppy feed.

By breakfast time the work was finished and Dannie and Martin were both ravenous.

Anna Wyn's call across the yard startled them.

"Tom Pritchard's on the phone. He wants to know if anyone's seen Tag. He's been out all night, and they don't know where he's gone."

Chapter 5

Tom Pritchard was on his way to Bryn Gwynt. Everyone was worried about Tag, wondering where the child could have gone, but for the moment there seemed nothing they could do about it. Martin ate, without noticing what he was eating, half his mind on Tag and the other half on Blue who had developed a problem.

The Jack Russell puppy that had been dumped on them, and adopted by Martin, had discovered its legs. At first it had been happy to crawl round the box, and stay beside its foster father. Now the big world outside beckoned. He had struggled over the edge of the bed, and flopped onto the floor. Blue, sure this was not allowed, promptly picked him up and put him back.

The pup needed to move. Every instinct told him he had to practise using his legs, and he squealed in a small rage which made everyone laugh.

The laughter puzzled the big dog. So did the insistence of his small charge on leaving the safety of his bed and venturing out onto the kitchen floor.

"It's OK, Blue," Martin said, as the big dog made another attempt to bring the pup back to the box. He whistled and Blue came to him and sat beside him, his ears flat against his head, leaning on his master's knee, a puzzled frown on his face.

"He's a lot to learn about pups," Anna Wyn said, as Tom Pritchard erupted through the door without knocking. Blue, occupied with guarding his tail against small teeth, looked up and recognized a friend.

"Look," Tom said. "When did you last see Tag?"

"Last night." Dannie poured a cup of coffee, and passed it across the table. "Sit down. He won't be far away. And he'll be OK. He's not stupid."

"I'm not so sure about that." Tom's American accent was suddenly much more pronounced. "It was a bad row. Tag neither forgives nor forgets easily."

"What happened?" Leah asked. She buttered a

slice of toast and spread it with marmalade. "Eat up. I bet you haven't had breakfast."

The puppy, having managed to negotiate the vast desert that was the kitchen floor, had reached Tom's trainers. Engrossed, he began to worry at the laces. Tom reached down and picked him up and held him tight. Blue growled. It was his puppy.

"It's OK, feller," Dannie said. "Nobody will hurt him. Have to get used to this, you know."

"Like our friends have to get used to a madhouse," Leah said. "Tom, what upset Tag?"

"His grandmother sent him a computer game from the States. Only it wouldn't work on his computer. Not compatible. We were out and he tried it on mine. It didn't work on that either. He blew six weeks' work; and I hadn't printed it out. All the last eight chapters of my book have gone. I'd been so busy writing I forgot to back up."

Most of this was gibberish to everyone in the room, but the thought of six weeks' lost work was understandable.

"So you were mad at him," Anna Wyn said. "I'm not surprised."

"Mad? I hit the roof. I told Tag a few home truths. I knew as I was doing it that I was going over the top, but I've got a deadline to keep."

"A deadline?" Leah looked at him, frowning.

She had been feeling for some minutes as if he were talking a strange tongue.

"My publisher wants the manuscript by the end of November. Now I've lost eight chapters, and I'll have to write them from scratch. I've got my notes, of course, but it never comes out as good the second time around. You lose the edge of interest."

"He was here, hiding in the barn around midnight," Dannie said. "I was helping Martin with a difficult calving: a breach. We hadn't time for him. I sent him packing. I wasn't easy on him either."

"Has he taken anything with him?" Martin asked, with an uneasy memory of his own attempt at running away two years before. He had fallen and hurt himself and Dannie had rescued him. Suppose Tag . . . Martin remembered only too vividly the misery that had caused him to run off, sure that nobody wanted him and that his stepfather hated him, and always blamed him for everything that went wrong on the farm.

It felt like a century ago. He had grown up so much since then.

"Has he taken anything with him?" Dannie repeated the question which Tom appeared not to have heard.

"Food. Whatever was in his money box. He had a cash box with a lock on it that he kept by his bed. That's open and empty. A spare set of clothes. His bicycle." Tom paused. When he spoke again, his voice was softer. "Little idiot. He could be anywhere. Where do we look? Do we tell the police? He might turn up at any time and it would be wasting police effort." He bit savagely at his toast. "Tag's never been an easy child. He's run off before, but he's always been back within a few hours."

Martin had another unhappy memory of his first meeting with Tag, who had only been six years old then. More than five years ago. The child had tried to pull a rock with a fossil in it out of a drystone wall, which had fallen on him and pinned him, breaking his arm. At least he wouldn't be looking for fossils this time. That had been for Mike, and Mike had long ago lost interest in his collection and passed it on to a friend.

"Where's Mike this weekend?"

"Camping with two friends near Ogwen. They're on call for Mountain Rescue."

The mountains attracted so many people, few of them ever dressed for the weather. Rain, fog, even snow came hurtling out of the clouds, and the Search and Rescue helicopter streaked across the sky, towards the killing hills.

Tag envied Mike. He envied Dannie. He even envied Martin. He couldn't wait to be grown up and do everything that they did. Suppose he had taken to the hills?

The Jack Russell pup, exhausted by his first adventure, had fallen asleep. Anna Wyn took him from Tom and laid him in the box. Blue, thankful to see his charge restored to him and behaving in a manner he had come to regard as normal, settled down beside the mite, and licked its head.

It half woke, yawned, tucked itself against the big dog, burrowing into his warmth, and fell asleep again. Blue laid his head on the edge of the box and looked at his family, knowing that something was wrong.

After a moment he left the box again and sat in front of Tom, looking up at the big man with a considering stare, before thoughtfully offering his paw. "You . . . " Tom said, but he took the paw and shook it, knowing the dog was trying to comfort him. He put his arm around Blue's shoulders.

"I'm ringing Dafydd the Police," Leah said. "We'll see what he has to say. He's due to collect his pup soon, so I can just mention Tag in passing."

Dafydd had little to say except that he was coming.

Martin looked uneasily at Dannie. They had the animals to feed and clean before ten o'clock and time was flying away. There was no way they could join in any search until late that evening, and by then, hopefully, Tag would be found.

"The boys have the farm work to do, and Gwyn's away," Leah said.

"I ought to be off. You go ahead." Tom stood up.

"Dafydd's coming here. You two get on with the work. Anna Wyn can go with you." Leah began to stack the dishes and clear the table. "I'll just get rid of these. The housework can wait."

Tom stared at his half-eaten toast. He drank his coffee in one gulp and then prowled round the room, unable to settle.

"Tag wouldn't do anything too stupid," Dannie said, as they worked fast, cleaning out the pig sties. Martin hooked the soiled straw onto the barrow and Dannie wheeled it off to the muck heap, which was well hidden right at the back of the Animal Park. Every few weeks in spring he drove up to the nursery with manure for their soil. In return the owner gave them free vegetables.

Martin wasn't so sure. Tag had a genius for getting himself into scrapes. He was always in trouble at school, often for the silliest things. Martin, busy brushing Caley, who had once belonged to Tag, felt unease growing in him. Caley, sensing that his groom was distracted, butted Martin with his head, so that he slipped and fell. The pony looked down at him as if amused by his success.

"You'll only have the nastiest children on your back today if you go on like that," Martin said, picking himself up off the ground. He'd have to change into clean clothes. He'd fallen in mud.

"Someone else having a bad day," Dafydd's voice said, amused. His radio was chattering into the air. He was a dapper man, who always seemed to Martin to be too small to be in uniform. "Where does young Tag like to go?"

"Almost anywhere. I used to know, but now he hardly ever comes here, except to talk to Dannie. He's no time for me, these days, unless he wants me to do something for him."

"Hero worshipper, is young Tag," said Dafydd, who knew all the villagers well.

Martin looked irritably at the pony. "He'll have to do. Lick and a promise. Taid would turn in his grave." He sighed suddenly. Dafydd was easy to talk to. "I still miss Taid. He always had time to listen, and he taught, without you knowing he was teaching."

"So he's still here, in all he taught you and everyone else," Dafydd said. "That's a good life. If only we could leave the same memories, we'd have done well."

"Tag . . . " Martin said, his voice forlorn. "Suppose . . . "

"That one'll be back. He bounces. And he'd talk his way out of anything. I wouldn't like to kidnap young Tag. He'd exhaust me long before

58

it was time to set him free. I'd let him go early rather than have to listen to him and answer all his questions."

"What do we do? Where do you look? He could be anywhere."

"We'll look, lad, believe you me. You've work to do." He glanced across the yard. "Here, if I'm not mistaken, are your first customers."

On any other day Martin would have been delighted to see the monstrous coach that drove into the yard. It was a double-decker, complete with bathroom, lounge, TV and heaven knew what else. It carried more people than they could cope with in so short a time; nothing was ready. The animals were only half fed, some of them not yet let out of their nighttime sheds.

And Gwyn wasn't yet back and Martin would have to lead them down the farm trail; and Dannie would have to cope as best he could, while Anna Wyn raced round to let everything out, and carry on with the feeding.

"Oh gee," said a very American voice. "Just look at this. Isn't it quaint?" A camera snapped, taking a picture of the farmhouse. "And are you one of the hands?" he asked, as Martin tried to get into the house to clean himself up, without being seen.

"I'm family," Martin said. "If you'll excuse me for two minutes, I fell in the mud."

Leah appeared at the door, smiling.

"We have to apologize," she said. "The young son of a friend of ours has gone missing. He got lost overnight, and we're behind hand. Would you all like to come into the tea room and have coffee and homemade scones, on the house, while Martin gets cleaned up and Dannie and Anna Wyn finish feeding the animals in the park."

There were murmurs of commiseration. Martin watched them troop away, and raced indoors, where he reckoned he could beat any stage act at the speed with which he shed his clothes and dressed again.

He had forgotten the polecat, but when he lookad at the cage, it was empty. He ran out to find Anna Wyn.

"I thought I might as well feed him when I fed the little Rotti pup," she said, seeing Martin's anxious face. "I thought you had enough on your plate." She smiled suddenly. "You're doing a grand job. Go on, and cope with the mob."

When he went across to the farm shop and tea room, the people from the coach were happily chatting to Leah, who was telling them about Anna Wyn's many invalids and orphans. She brought the Jack Russell pup out to show them, with Blue trotting anxiously behind, afraid it was being taken away from him.

She handed it to an elderly lady whose blue hair curled in close ringlets against her head.

While others clustered round, Leah managed to whisper to Martin.

"I'll do the first farm trail. There are so many of them we'll have to split them into four groups. It won't be the way Gwyn does it, but I can manage to interest them. I'll concentrate on the animals. You go and help Dannie. And here's their entry money."

It was a wonderful start to the day, and if it hadn't been for Tag, Martin would have been overjoyed. As it was the worry niggled at him all morning.

Jennet came in late, and apologized.

"Dafydd kept me. He thought I might know all Tag's favourite places. I knew some . . . he wasn't in any of them. His mother's so worried . . . "

She was unusually silent, which made the day feel even more strange. Jennet usually babbled. The Pritchard's caravan was on Jennet's family's land, and the two families were very close to one another as friends as well as neighbours.

The Americans were fascinated and overwhelming, interested in everything they saw. They clucked at the pheasant with his wing strapped up, and laughed at Stuart the seagull, who still thought shoelaces were worms and devoted his attention to anyone who wore them.

The visitors decided they would rather have homemade sandwiches than lunch anywhere else.

The courier went to the phone and cancelled the rest of the day. They were due to visit Beaumaris Castle, but everyone was captivated by the peace, and the view of the mountains on the mainland.

They sat in the sun at the picnic tables, and drank coffee and enthused over Leah's home-made crusty new bread, roast ham, and farm butter and cheese made from ewes' milk.

Her walnut cake produced several requests for the recipe, which Leah now had photocopied so that those asking could take it home with them without the need for her to write it out.

Two of the men were intrigued by the Noah's Ark.

"Did you make it yourselves?" they asked. Martin nodded.

"It took all winter. We had help with the shell of the little house, but Dannie and I did the decorating and put the shelves up and made the tables and stools. Laura, a friend of ours, painted them."

The tables were bright blue, and the matching stools were decorated with pictures of animals. Animal posters hung on the walls, covering every inch. Elephants and seals, charts of dog breeds and cat breeds, pictures of puppies and kittens, of fieldmice and flying owls; hovering kestrels and a painted dragon.

The shelves were filled with Dannie's wooden

animals, all in pairs. A brightly painted ladder led from the ground to the little door, and the children adored it.

Not only was the Ark photographed, but one of the members of the coach party had a video camera and the smallest ladies were invited to climb the ladder and sit inside. There was no time for Martin and Dannie to stop for lunch.

Jennet brought them coffee and sandwiches and took a turn at the desk, while Martin hid himself behind Hannah's sty to give himself time to at least eat a quick snack. Dannie had perfected the art of eating on the run. Jennet was sure it wasn't good for any of them, but was too busy herself to do more than try and fill in and give them a breathing space.

"I think it's the loveliest place," one of the American ladies said. "It's so tiny but there's so much here."

Martin had a sudden forlorn image of Tag bragging: "America's big. This country's like a cabbage patch."

When the coach finally drove away Martin raced across the yard and into the kitchen, where Leah was washing up a mountain of dishes.

"I never thought I'd cope. I had to de-freeze piles of scones, another two cakes, and four more loaves. Thank heaven for the new big deep freeze and the microwave. Last year I'd have had to say, "Sorry, sold out.""

"Any news of Tag?" Martin asked.

"No news at all."

The day lost all brightness and in spite of the sun, Martin suddenly felt cold.

Chapter 6

At last the animals and birds were fed and watered and cleaned out. The cages and sheds were locked for the night. Martin had felt that the day would never end.

There was no news of Tag.

"Food before you join the search," Leah said.

Martin, Jennet and Dannie ate fast, not tasting their meal at all, their minds on the boy. Where had he gone? What had happened to him? Nobody spoke.

"I'll search here," Dannie said, when they had finished eating. "He might be hiding in one of the hay lofts; or the barns; and the old outbuildings have all kinds of crannies. He might have fallen and hurt himself."

"Trust Tag," Jennet said. "He's always doing something daft, but this beats all. So where do we hunt?"

"I know some of his favourite walks," Martin said. "I'll take Blue; maybe he could track him."

Gwyn, walking into the kitchen, stared at them.

"It's nice to be greeted," he said. "Didn't any of you hear me come? Don't you want to see our newcomers?

"Tag's run away," Leah said. "No one's seen him for twenty-four hours."

Gwyn sat down in his chair. Blue came to greet him, and was rewarded with an absent-minded pat. "Have the police been told?"

"Yes." Dannie stood up. "I'm going to search round here. He was in the byre last night. Merry had her calf."

"Is it OK?"

"It's fine. Heifer calf." Which meant they kept her for breeding. A bull calf would be sold. Time enough to tell Gwyn later about the problem they had had. "Tag popped out of the straw just as we were starting; it was midnight and we sent him home. It was daft now I come to think of it. Anyone might have picked him up. Nobody would be about to see."

Anna Wyn came back into the kitchen.

"Laura was coming tonight for a fitting for our wedding dresses. I rang to put her off, but she'd forgotten anyway. She and Mike are both out searching. Mike wondered if Tag had gone climbing. He always wants to do what the rest of us do."

Death lurked in the mountains, always ready to trap the unwary and the careless. Martin, going out into the yard with Blue at his side, stared up at the lowering tops, at Tryfan, the most notorious, who, legend said, required a death a year. Often there were more than that. People slipped and fell. They wore the wrong clothes and the wrong kind of shoes, and failed to respect the dangers of the high hills.

Bryn Gwynt was on the flight path for the Search and Rescue helicopters. Sometimes at night, when rain lashed against his bedroom window, Martin woke and heard the heart-stopping beat of the engines and knew that another climber was lost.

The worst accidents always seemed to happen when the wind screamed down the crevices, and ice formed on rock and hair and skin. Martin could cuddle into his bedclothes and shiver as he thought of those lying out in need of help. The men flew on. No bed for them that night until the victim was safe in hospital, or if the worst came to the worst, lay in the morgue.

He prayed that Tag hadn't tried to climb in the mountains

Martin had lost the desire to climb. He was

becoming as passionate about the animals as the rest of the family. If only Tag would settle down and be sensible. Would the boy ever learn? It was hard, being twelve. But not all twelve year olds were like Tag.

Few had his curiosity, his desire to find out. Or his fury when his strength did not match his desires, or his intense longing to do as Martin and Dannie and Mike did, and not spend his time with boys of his own age.

Tag hated being curbed, hated obeying rules, hated being unable to drive a car, or ride a motorbike. He behaved as if he would never have time to grow up, never have time to learn all the skills as an adult. Maybe he knew something they didn't and his life was going to be cut short.

Martin tried to change the direction of his thoughts, but his mind disobeyed him and ran away with ideas that became more and more terrifying. Tag, come home you little ass, he thought, wishing that a thought could become a command, a yell, an imperative cry that the boy would hear and obey.

Martin's thoughts raced on. Tag had been wearing summer clothes, not even an anorak or jersey. Hopefully he had gone home and remedied that. Summer nights could be very cold and one year there had been snow on the mountain tops in August.

"Tag, you little fool," Martin said aloud. The

worry flared into an ache, and an unexpected searing guilt. If only he and Dannie hadn't sent the boy away . . . If they had only thought . . . If only. Saddest words in any language, Taid's voice said in the darkness.

If only Taid were there, to talk, to comfort.

Why was life so difficult?

He walked down the village street, up onto the moorland above Mervyn's farm, now sold. Strangers lived in the house and the fields were rented by various farmers for their sheep. The newcomers wouldn't know Tag. Martin looked down at the farmhouse, now bright with new paint. The outbuildings had been pulled down. They were almost derelict anyway. Only a neat garage and Tag wouldn't be in there. The yard had become a garden.

Mervyn now lived in a little bungalow on a sheltered housing estate. He missed the farm and was still a frequent visitor to Bryn Gwynt. But he hadn't Taid's talent for listening. Martin had a sudden need to go to the old man's grave, to sit there and talk to him as if he were alive.

He had to find Tag. He had to distract his thoughts. He looked down at the unfamiliar place that had once been Plas Towyn, and well known to him.

He walked down the path and across the garden that had been a cobbled yard.

Once Hero the bull had rampaged behind the

farmhouse, and pinned his master to the wall. Martin and Blue had saved the old man's life.

He knocked at the door which was answered by a sour looking boy with a black eye.

"What do you want?"

"We're looking for a boy of twelve. He hasn't called here?"

"No."

The door slammed shut in his face. The newcomers came from England, as Martin and his mother had. Maybe they would become part of the village one day. Maybe never. He called to Blue, who was investigating the outside of a rabbit hole with great interest. He climbed back up the hill.

The wind teased at his hair.

Where could Tag have gone?

Up the craggy path towards Megan the Lump, where her tiny cottage sheltered under a huge rock outcrop down which water poured.

Megan was standing at her gate. She looked so tiny now. Martin paused to greet her. "Dafydd the Police was here," she said, knowing Martin would understand. "Is there any news?"

Martin shook his head.

"I can't even think of any place to search."

He had a sudden memory of himself, two years ago, running away, sure no one wanted him. This was how the family would have felt. How could he have been so stupid? He would feel concerned about someone he only knew slightly, but Tag was part of his life, even though at times, a maddening part. His parents were half demented with worry.

Martin's mind was full of memories of the boy. Tag with his lopsided grin, his hair that never lay flat, the bright bush standing up on the crown. Tag with his stormy tantrums and his sudden passions that never lasted. Tag trying to ride Caley, and falling off. Tag, suddenly tender with a new kitten, unable to believe it was so small.

"It's so stupid," Martin said angrily. "We're so helpless. He could have cycled to the mainland, and then on to Llanberis. He's always talking about climbing by moonlight, like Mike."

"Precious little moon at the moment," Megan said. "Clouds and rain every night. No light at all." She frowned. "We'd know if he'd had an accident. The police will have made enquiries at the hospitals."

"He may have fallen. But where? Or gone swimming and been drowned."

Megan was too old to think that every adventure had a happy ending. Few people thought that these days, with so many disastrous stories every night on the news. She led the way through the gate and up her garden path.

The evening light was fading. Tag had been out for the whole of the night before, and now another night was on them, and angry clouds were building on the hills. Anvil-shaped clouds, towering high, threatening a storm.

"Come in and have a coffee with me," Megan said. "Little use hunting in the dark. It will only add to everyone's worry if you fail to go home."

Martin wanted to refuse the drink, but Megan was lonely, and he owed her a great deal. She had taught him Welsh, which had made school life bearable. He was still not very good, but he knew enough to understand what was said to him and mostly to answer. He could carry on a conversation at home, when Gwyn and the girls remembered that he and his mother were not yet fluent, and slowed their speech.

He signed to Blue to lie down in the doorway and ducked his head as he went inside.

Megan grinned.

"First time," she said. Martin laughed. It had taken months of banging his head before he remembered he was now taller than the doorway that once he had walked through so easily.

"I had permanent lumps on my head," he said.

The cottage too seemed to have shrunk. The big black cat had died. Megan had rescued another, very similar to her lost pet. She came to greet him, rubbing round his legs and purring. She knew him well. She returned to the back of the settee, where she lay, looking at him through slitted eyes. Her paws kneaded the wool of the brightly crocheted cover.

"He's just vanished," Martin said.

Megan sighed.

"They'll find him. Probably somewhere near."

The thought came to both of them.

St David's cave.

The cave was behind the Lump, the vast bluff that towered above the cottage. It was a tiny place that might shelter a child. Martin raced round the rock, calling to Blue, calling to Tag, his voice echoing.

Megan, limping after him, brought a big hand-lamp. He had forgotten how dark it was inside.

The rays of the lamp showed nothing but dead leaves and dark walls dripping with moisture. Nobody had been there for a long time.

Martin had been so sure. He stood up, and stared at the darkened mountains, wondering what secrets they hid. Megan put a hand on his arm.

"Best get back," she said. "You don't want to add to their worries. Go by the road. The moorland paths are treacherous in the dark. Take my torch. Bring it back tomorrow, you can have your coffee then."

It was longer by road. It was nearly midnight when Martin got in. Gwyn was sitting in the big armchair, the Jack Russell puppy on his knee. Spider and Ginger, the two rescued cats, lay curled on the rug.

There was a big box in the corner of the

73

kitchen, near the Aga. Martin looked inside and saw the polecat kitten cuddled up against the tiny Rottweiler pup.

"They're the same age and both lonely for their mothers and their sisters and brothers," Anna Wyn said. "Seemed sensible."

Martin looked at his stepfather.

"I give up," Gwyn said. "I decided on my way home I'd rather have lunatic children who rescue everything in sight than stupid yobs getting into trouble all the time."

Martin had room for only one thought: "No news?"

Gwyn shook his head.

"He's vanished into thin air." His hand stroked the pup's head. Blue came up to the farmer, and firmly took the puppy in his mouth. He marched across to his box, knowing that was where all dogs slept, and it was long after their usual bedtime. The puppy licked the big dog's face, and moaned with pleasure as he snuggled against his protector.

"Your mother's gone to stay with the Pritchards. They're in a bad way. Midge isn't helping. She likes being the centre of attention and now she isn't. She reckons Tag's done it on purpose to spite her."

"Midge is a pain."

Martin, suddenly hungry, cut himself a thick slice of new baked bread and buttered it.

"Anna Wyn left you some soup. It only needs a minute in the microwave."

Martin heated his soup and sat drinking it, his mind still on Tag. Then he remembered Gwyn had been away.

"Did you have a good trip?"

"Very. I've brought several animals for the Park. Expected everyone to be overjoyed, but that's life. Always turns round and hits you, just when everything seems to be going well."

Martin forced himself to concentrate.

"What did you buy?"

"Two miniature ponies. A couple of pygmy goats. And an early wedding present for both girls."

Martin had forgotten the weddings.

"Come and see."

Gwyn led the way to the yard, and then to one of the smaller sheds. Inside, on a table, was a large cage, in which lay two Burmese kittens, curled up closely, their paws around each other.

One was a golden tan, the other a rich tortoise-shell.

"Are they pleased?"

"They haven't seen them yet. Dilys and Tony went out in their car to see if they could find any news of the child. Dannie and Anna Wyn took the Land Rover. They all came in late and very tired and unhappy. They'd called on the Pritchards to see if they had news. It didn't seem the right time to tell them, but I had to tell someone."

The kittens were sound asleep.

"They were very restless at first, but after I fed them they settled. Both girls want to breed Burmese. I've always said no. Enough to do. But I saw these two and thought they'd be enchanted."

Martin was sure they'd both be delighted.

Gwyn switched off the light and closed the door. Martin, lying in bed, found sleep refused to come. Instead he had visions of Tag, fallen down a crevasse, lying injured and cold, dying of hypothermia. Or run over, lying undiscovered in some ditch.

His alarm woke him at two a.m and he went down to the silent kitchen, to switch on the light and make up the feed for the two small animals. Anna Wyn had promised to feed them at four o'clock and his mother would be up at six.

Blue watched him, but preferred the comfort of his bed. He nosed the Jack Russell. It was odd, in the sleeping house, to be awake and sitting feeding milk to an animal so tiny that it fitted into the palm of his hand. The small bright eyes watched him, and he knew a brief moment of exhilaration as he thought of the trust that the orphans gave them.

The little Rottweiler was stronger. He lay on his back, four paws in the air, his small face wise.

"I reckon you know a lot of things I don't," Martin said, as he put the tiny animal back in its bed, and watched it cuddle up against its improbable companion. The polecat kitten thrust his nose into the pup's tummy, and before Martin had time to switch off the light, both small animals were asleep.

The presence of a companion might make the pup struggle harder to live.

The owls, calling mournfully to one another across the fields, did nothing to soothe his worries.

"Please God," he said into the darkness, "let Tag be safe. Please."

He trod quietly up the stairs to his bed, but sleep was no friend. He dreamed that he and Blue were tracking through the woods, and far away the small figure of a boy ran and ran and ran, and they never caught up with him.

Chapter 7

Martin woke in the night to hear thunder rumbling over the hills. Lightning split the sky. Zigzag streaks flashed across the ceiling. Blue hated storms. Martin put on his slippers and went downstairs.

Blue stared at him. The dog was lying in his bed, the pup cuddled against him. The big German Shepherd appeared to be trying to control his own fear for the sake of the baby. Martin put on the kettle, and watched the storm swirl across the hills.

Where was Tag? Out in the rain and the dark? Or sheltering somewhere, safe? Maybe he had gone to London and was hiding in cardboard city. He was daft enough.

Maybe he had accepted a lift, or hitchhiked. Maybe he had met with danger and failed to recognize it. Tag was trusting, and seldom remembered what he had been told.

Fear dried Martin's mouth. He began to pray, not even aware that he was praying. If only he could bargain with God. If only Tag was safe. If only . . .

There was a flash and a crack and tremendous rush of water. A deafening roar. Blue leaped out of his bed and the Jack Russell pup, terrified, sat shivering. Martin picked it up and went to the window. Rain streamed down it. He had never seen such rain. One second outside and any unfortunate would be drenched.

"Lightning hit the old tree. It's split it in two," Gwyn said from the doorway, making Martin jump. "Kettle on? Good. We'll probably end with a party."

Anna Wyn was next to come down.

"Was that the farmhouse hit?" she asked.

"The old tree." Gwyn switched on the yard lights. "Luckily it's fallen clear of every building. Just missed Caley's shelter."

The pony was thudding his hooves in terror against the stable door. There was no way they could reach him till morning. The tree blocked the yard. Worry flared in Anna Wyn's eyes.

"He'll hurt himself."

"He's plenty of room. Nothing we can do."

Gwyn said. "The tree's right across the path. Impossible to move till tomorrow. I saw it in a lightning flash."

Dilys, following on her sister's heels, was about to speak when lightning sparked again, followed by drumrolls that reverberated from the hills, echoing and re-echoing. All the lights went out.

"Wonder how Leah is getting on up at the Pritchards," Gwyn said. "She felt she had to stay with them."

It was odd without his mother, Martin thought. They hardly ever seemed to have time to speak to one another, except for mundane conversation, in passing, yet her absence left a most tremendous gap.

Rain fell out of the sky, drumming on the ground, surging against the windows. The night was crazy with noise. Blue dumped the puppy on Martin's knees and leaned against his master, asking for comfort and sanctuary in a world gone mad. The pup, scrabbling for balance, curled up in a small tight ball under Martin's dressing gown. Blue lay with his head against Martin's legs, pressing tightly as if sure that would bring him safety.

"Was that us that was hit?" Dilys sounded frightened. "Or Taid's cottage?"

"Neither," said Dannie's voice from the doorway. "I checked. Got soaked in the effort. Probably a power line gone." He came into the room, and shook his raincoat. "Anyone got a pair of dry pyjamas to lend me?"

Anna Wyn went to the ironing basket. Dannie took the crumpled objects and a towel and vanished briefly, to return, laughing, with both jacket and trousers far too short. The bright stripes were topped by one of Gwyn's oldest jerseys, loose and full of holes. His hair stood up in a shaggy bush all round his head. He poured hot water into a mug in which Dilys had mixed milk and cocoa.

"What a night. All the legions of hell gone fighting."

And Tag out there in the darkness, Martin thought but didn't say it aloud. "I hope the rain eases by milking time." Gwyn's face was sombre, lit by the beam of a large handlamp that Leah set on the table. "I'm glad we have an Aga. At least we can have hot drinks and some hot food."

They sat, all drinking cocoa, which Dilys had decided was more appropriate than coffee in the middle of the night. Anna Wyn was worrying about her animals. Caley still thumped an angry hoof against the stable wall. Outside in the tormented trees the birds were crying.

"Rain's eased," Gwyn said, half an hour later, when the thunder was only a distant growl and everyone was yawning. He borrowed Dannie's torch and went out into the darkness. He returned in a few minutes with the cage that Martin had seen. The kittens clung together, their eyes terrified.

Gwyn put the cage on the table.

"Part of your wedding presents," he said. "Don't fight over them. One each. I wanted to fetch them before, poor mites. The noise must have been frightened them beyond reason."

The girls looked at them in disbelief. Anna Wyn opened the cage, lifted out the golden kitten, and held it against her. It burrowed into her dressing gown.

Dilys's kitten was bolder. She sat on her new mistress's knee, considering her from bright greeny-yellow eyes.

"They're adorable."

"They're well bred, I'm told," Gwyn said. "Might make a little money for each of you when they have kittens. I have their pedigrees."

"Maybe we could show them." Dilys picked up the end of her dressing gown sash and wriggled it. The kitten, forgetting the noise and her fear, put out a tentative paw and tapped it. As it swung in the air, she caught it, worried it and let it go.

"Are they Siamese?" Dannie asked.

"Burmese," Gwyn said.

Anna Wyn's kitten settled to sleep in the warm darkness. She had no intention of coming out into the light to be looked at. The girls went to bed.

"Let them sleep," Gwyn said. "We've work to do. I had a quick look round the Sanctuary.

The Shetlands panicked and broke their door down. The pig enclosure's flooded. And Moggles has decided to have twins, and you know what she's like."

They could hear the cow's anxious bawling above the sounds of the night.

"Not much we can do yet for her. Better get on with making the animals safe."

The rumbling thunder accompanied them as they struggled to re-assure the ponies. Lightning flared and flamed on the far hills, lighting them briefly and leaving the sky even blacker than before.

The lull was momentary as the storm returned and rain lashed down, soaking them.

Blue, brought out to help shift the pigs to safer quarters, soon looked like a drowned rat. Martin gave up trying to keep dry. He squelched forlornly through the mud, picking up frantic flapping geese that had tried to find shelter when the wind blew their shed down.

A hideous squawk told him that the peacock was also adrift, and it was ten minutes before he found the bird crouching under a hedge, its back to the wind.

At the back of his mind the worry about Tag flared and then diminished as he found yet another victim of the storm.

Daylight came, grey and dismal, the rain easing to a fine drizzle.

"Shower and change before milking. No use even trying to go to bed," Gwyn said, yawning. Rain had plastered his hair against his head, and his soaked clothes clung to him. Martin knew he looked as odd. Dannie stood and wrung the water out of his sleeves.

"Twins OK?" he asked.

Martin had forgotten about Moggles.

"Come and look." Gwyn yawned again, a massive yawn that Martin thought would dislocate his jaw. A moment later he and Dannie were also yawning, and Martin grinned as Blue, shaking himself, yawned too. "Thought they might be orphans of the storm," Gwyn said. "But she's OK."

"But one of the calves is red and white. Moggles is Friesian and so was the bull," Martin said.

"It's a throwback. All Friesians were red and white or black and white when they were imported, centuries ago." Gwyn yawned again. "Odd that only one calf has that colouring. Be a big attraction, I shouldn't wonder. Come on, let's get dry."

Thunder was still rumbling in the distance. Gwyn yawned and went up to change. Dannie vanished. Martin looked at his dog. He dropped his soaked clothes on the kitchen floor and draped a towel round himself, and then began to dry Blue. There was no way he could make himself comfortable and leave a drenched animal to dry out on his own.

He lined the dog box with towels, and moved the pup to another bed. Upstairs, he glanced into the polecat's cage, but it was empty. Anna Wyn had taken over for the night and he was grateful. He had forgotten all about the two-hourly feeds.

Dressed, he went out into a drowned world and stared at the desolation. More work. If it wasn't one thing, it was another. The wind had torn off roofing. They would have to build stronger enclosures. If only the sun would come out and the place could dry.

If only he could go to be and sleep for a week. Nobody had mentioned Tag, but he knew that they all had been thinking of the child.

Was Tag afraid of thunder? He couldn't fail to be if out of doors. Nobody could stay calm with that din overhead. He'd be soaked to the skin, lying somewhere curled in the darkness, while the sky seethed and flamed above him.

Wearily, Martin went into the yard. The generator was thumping.

Dannie, the chainsaw in his hand, attacked the fallen tree.

"Dilys is helping Gwyn with the milking. We need to get this out of the way quickly, so that we can reach Caley. Also there's a dickens of a lot of tidying up to do before the visitors start to arrive. The sand pit's flooded. We'll have to cover it or some small fry will be getting themselves in a right mess and mums won't like that."

It was still raining. A persistent downfall, though not nearly as heavy as it had been during the night.

"It'll be a brave family who venture out today," Martin said. He hoped it would be a quiet day. They needed time to remedy the storm damage.

"Always something," Gwyn said, as he called Blue to help lead the cattle back to the field.

The logs were piling up. It had been a big tree. Martin piled wood behind the barn, helped by Gwyn and Leah and Anna Wyn.

"Need help?" Jennet asked, a small grin on her face. Nobody had seen her arrive. "Need I ask?"

She brought the wheelbarrow to Martin and helped him stack the logs. She trundled it away, her small figure determined.

They had just finished when the milk lorry came.

"Tidy old mess everywhere," the driver said, as he prepared to take the milk into the tanker. "Cottage in the village struck last night. No news of the boy I don't suppose?"

"Not so far as we know." Dannie sat wearily on the bench outside the kitchen window. "Not the best way to start the day is it. Better see how that pony is, Martin."

Caley was frightened and irritable. He was also

exhausted. He had banged away for half the night and nobody had come to him.

Martin soothed him and groomed him. Caley tossed his head and stamped his foot, and then, irritated beyond measure by a world he didn't understand that had blazed at him and deafened him, he neatly nipped the top button off Martin's shirt. Martin, trying to retrieve it before it was swallowed, got nipped himself.

The pony wouldn't be fit to ride if any visitors did arrive. Both the Shetlands were in foal, so they couldn't be ridden either.

Breakfast was a silent meal, with everyone engrossed in their own thoughts. The Burmese kittens had been fed and put back in their cage, to keep them safe. They weren't used to the place and might get into the yard and be run over when visitors came.

They were also eminently stealable.

"Not a sanctuary attraction," Anna Wyn said. "At least, not roaming free. The World of Birds had some of their attractions stolen. I dont want that to happen. I wish Taid were here. He could have built them a big pen, out of sight, round the back. Nobody has time to do it."

Spider, walking in through the kitchen door, saw the cage on the table and sprang up to investigate. His fur fluffed and he spat in fury. Two midget kits fluffed and spat in return.

"They'll have to learn to like one another. But

not yet. The poor little things need to get used to us and probably to recover from last night's mayhem."

Rain had drenched the hanging baskets. Broken stems lay in all the flowerbeds, and twigs littered the grass. Yesterday's bright blooms looked as if they had been trampled by a herd of cows.

"One step forward, ten steps back," Martin said. "It looks a tip. No one would think we'd done any work here at all."

"Where's Jennet?" Anna Wyn asked a few minutes later. "I asked her to put water in all the pens and cages and sties, but she's vanished. She won't be any use at all if she does that."

Grudgingly, Martin took over the watering. He always meant to count the number of times he filled the two cans, but in the end lost count halfway through. A million treks from tap to container. He was bone tired and his legs began to ache. The pigs, thirsty, raced at him, and both buckets were spilled.

As he tramped back through the mud, a truck pulled into the yard, and Jennet called to him from the passenger window.

"I've brought a rescue gang." Her uncle and her cousin Mike and two friends leaped out. The back of the truck was filled with flowers and greenery. "Dad's lending you some displays; they'll help tide you over till we get sorted again."

Martin glanced at his stepsister.

"Now I feel mean," she whispered.

"You couldn't know," he whispered back.

Willing hands were uprooting damaged flowers. Jennet's uncle took down the hanging baskets and replaced them.

"I can replant these for you. Got a lot of stuff left over that I haven't sold. Be glad to get rid of it," he said.

Mike yawned.

"We were out on the mountains half the night," he said. "Some one was caught in the storm; fell on the track down Snowdon and slipped. Broken arm and head injuries. "

"Who's looking for Tag?" Martin asked.

"Everyone, I hope. Trouble is he could be anywhere. You know Tag."

They were silent as they worked, all of them wondering about the boy. The generator thumped in the background, until just after eleven when the power came back on.

The wind still shouted in the trees and grey clouds rushed overhead, promising more rain. There was little likelihood of visitors today, and Martin breathed a sigh of relief. At least they would have time to remedy the storm damage, without interruption.

By midday everything was as tidy as was possible, the last branches of the tree removed, and the flowerbeds brave with new bedding plants. There was little they could do about the wet ground. Martin covered the flooded sandpit with netting.

"We can break for lunch at one," Dannie said. Everyone else had gone. Jennet was busy cleaning the aviaries. Anna Wyn was tending her invalids. Leah was still with the Pritchards, who, Jennet's uncle said, were in a bad way, completely distraught with worry.

"Half-past twelve," Dannie said. "Time for a little more tidying up. The wind took part of the roof off the goat shed. I'd better get down to repairing it, or that'll leak." Martin was about to check the ark when he heard a sound behind him. Midge stood there, her eyes desolate, her face streaked with tears.

"I can't bear it," she said.

"Hey, hey," Dannie looked at her. "They'll find him, girl. Don't worry. Tag always comes up smiling, no matter what happens to him."

"It's Mom . . . she can't take it. I've never seen her like this . . . she can't cope at all. If Leah hadn't come, I don't know what they'd have done. I'm no use. They don't even see me. All they can think about is Tag. Stupid little beast . . . why didn't he think?"

"Dont sympathize," Dannie whispered to Martin as Midge walked outside. "*She* won't be able to cope if you do. She cares only she can't show it. We have to be brisk; give her something to do, or she'll fall apart too."

They followed her into the yard.

"Can I help? I've got to do something . . . I can't just go on thinking . . . or watching Mom and Dad . . . It's all wrong . . . I thought they were so strong."

"Ask someone to bring me some sandwiches," Gwyn called from the cow byre. "Sally's started calving. Can't leave her. She always has problems."

"I don't believe it," Dannie said, as a musical horn sounded gaily.

Martin turned towards the gate. One of the big American coaches was manoeuvreing into the yard, and it was full of people.

They watched, mesmerized, as it stopped and the courier climbed out. She smiled at them, a pretty blonde woman, very little older than Anna Wyn, dressed in a pale blue suit, and wearing a little forage cap set jauntily on the side of her head.

"We ordered lunch for forty people," she said. "It doesn't look the best of days to walk around so maybe we can eat first and then those that want to follow the Trail can do so afterwards?"

Dannie stared at Martin. Jennet, joining them, looked helplessly at Midge.

"Sure," Dannie said, rallying. "Would you like to take everyone into the tea room? I'll tell them you're here."

"Tell who? You're mad," Martin said, watching

people spill over the yard, looking for the toilets and exclaiming at the quaintness.

"It's that American firm. They've booked in here regularly, as everyone was so thrilled with the place last year. I'd completely forgotten they were due today. I bet Leah has too. If we let them down the word will spread. Come on, Midge. Work to do."

Midge, startled out of her misery, raced after them into the kitchen.

"What's Leah put in the daybook?" Jennet walked over to look. "Nothing. Either she forgot to or they've come on the wrong day. Now what do we do?"

Chapter 8

"This needs very fast thinking," Dannie said. "We have to give them something. We can't send them away. What do we do?"

"Tell them we're disorganized," Martin suggested. "Ask them to forgive us. Tell them why. After all, they're all Americans and so is Tag."

"Your job," Dannie said. "Give them a talk. Sing comic songs. Dance. Take Caley in and ride bareback. Do anything only for Pete's sake, give us time. Jennet, borrow my moped, and down to the Bryn stores. All the sliced loaves you can carry; butter; ham, tongue. Use your wits, girl, and don't let us down, please."

"Tell him why and that we'll pay tomorrow," Anna Wyn said. "We haven't nearly enough in the kitty."

Martin watched until the last visitor had gone into the converted barn. His mouth dry, he walked over. He had never had to talk to so large a group before, or in such circumstances.

A chuckle went up as he came in, and he stood, embarrassed, wondering what had made them laugh. Something butted his knee agitatedly. He stared down at Blue, who was offering him the puppy, obviously desperate.

"You take the wretched thing," his attitude said. The pup had decided to explore the yard, as someone had left the kitchen door open. Blue was determined not to let his protégé stray. He had made the dismaying discovery that the puppy had far more energy than any large dog. This one also had far more determination. Worse, Blue couldn't understand why it had been easy to carry his charge a week ago, but now it was extremely difficult as the pup had mysteriously become much heavier.

The pup surprised the big dog by being increasingly vocal, too, squealing in frustration every time Blue picked him up. The German Shepherd was exhausted.

"Nice dog," an amused voice said. "Handsome. Do you show him? Is that his pup? Blotted his copybook with a village mutt?"

A woman near to him held out her arms and Martin thankfully surrendered his charge, which snuggled trustingly into this new person's neck. Martin looked round at the smiling faces.

"Blue has no papers; he came to us out of a storm like last night's, several years ago. I train him, but can't show him. He knows how to find a missing person, though; and to hunt for things I've lost." Martin wasn't at all sure that any of his visitors would understand what he was talking about. "You can't show a dog without a written pedigree in this country. Someone dumped the pup on us. There were four of them, but the other three died. People often bring us puppies to handrear. He's a Jack Russell . . . little terrier."

"Say," said a man's voice, "do you often get animals dumped like that?"

"All the time. We've got a Rottweiler puppy now. Whenever there's a dog bite story a lot of owners get scared and simply throw the pups away. That makes it worse than ever, of course." Martin decided not to elaborate or he'd lose his temper. He wished he weren't so very tired. He hoped the two orphans hadn't been forgotten.

"Anna Wyn, my . . . " he hesitated. Stepsister was a mouthful. "My sister, she runs the Animal Park but half the time we have more rescued animals than well ones there. People bring us injured foxes and pheasants; oiled seabirds, and poisoned seabirds. Most of our rabbits were family pets whose owners got tired of them."

He looked around, afraid he was boring his

audience, but everyone seemed interested.

"My other sister is a veterinary nurse, engaged to a vet . . . "

"A vet?" The questioner sounded surprised.

"A veterinary surgeon; looks after sick animals." Tag used another word, but Martin couldn't remember it.

"Oh. You mean a veterinarian. In our country a vet is an old soldier, back from the war."

You have such silly words, Tag's voice said in his ear, complaining when he had got something wrong again. Oh Tag, blow you, Martin said inside his head. It's bad enough you disappearing without your voice creeping into my mind. Go away.

Only the fear wouldn't go away. It flared into sudden urgency as if Tag were calling to him for help.

"I have to make an apology," Martin said. Words were more difficult to find than he had imagined. "We hope you'll forgive us for keeping you waiting. Coffee will be coming, free, but the food may be a little while longer. A boy who lives in the village is missing; he's been lost for two nights and a day; this is the second day. Everyone who can is out looking for him. So we're very short handed."

"Poor little fellow," a comfortable voice said from the far end of the room. "Is he very little?"

"He's twelve. His name's Tag. His parents are

Americans too, over here to write a book."

"How did he get lost?" a man asked.

"He ran away. He'd meddled with his dad's computer and his dad was mad at him. Tag doesn't like anyone telling him off."

"What an odd name," said a young voice from the middle of the room.

"It's not his real name. I've forgotten what that is. We all call him Tag. When he was little he tagged on to anyone he fancied. Mike, from next door -- till he grew up and started work -- then me, and then Dannie who works here and is engaged to the sister who runs the Park."

"Are you Welsh?" someone asked. "You don't sound it."

"I was born in England. My mother married again nearly five years ago, so my new family is Welsh."

"Do you speak it?"

"Enough to get by."

"Can you say the place with the long name?" somebody asked.

Martin laughed.

"I think so, though I might leave out a bit. We call it Llanfair P.G. No one has time to say it all."

"Say it." It was a chorus.

Martin took a deep breath. How had he got into this? But it would fill up time. Jennet was handing round cups of coffee already. She grinned

at him. "Llanfairpwllgwyngyllgogerychwyrndrob-
wllllantysiliogogogoch." He took another deep
breath and grinned at them. "I don't think I've
left any of it out."

"I don't believe it," the woman holding the
puppy said. "What does it mean?"

"I think it means the church of St Mary's church
down by the wishing well, or something like that.
The story is it was invented by a parson in the
last century as a tourist attraction. Nobody really
knows." Martin wasn't at all sure of his facts.
Jennet patted him on the shoulder and whispered
"Good show."

Tne woman with the puppy smiled down at her
charge who had curled up trustingly and gone to
sleep. "How old is he?"

"The pup? About five weeks, we think. Can't
be certain. Our village policeman is taking him as
a pet for his wife."

Blue, who had flopped down, exhausted, raised
his head and stared at the woman holding the little
animal. He decided that all was well, and closed
his eyes, sighing deeply. A chuckle went round
the room.

Martin, now happy with his audience, kept one
eye on the door, wishing that the girls would
hurry with the food. He was running out of
things to say.

"How old is the farm?" someone asked.

"The farmhouse is seventeenth century in the

oldest part but it's been added to. Some is less than fifty years old. This barn is a historic monument; so we couldn't pull it down even if we wanted to, which we don't."

Jennet and Midge and Anna Wyn appeared with huge trays and began to lay food out on the long trestle tables. They were covered in bright cloths. Martin stared in disbelief at the food. Quiches and plates of cut turkey; huge bowls of green salad; hot garlic bread; all kinds of cheeses; bowls of apples and pears and bananas and grapes; an enormous glass bowl of fruit salad; jugs of cream; plates of sliced ham and tongue; bowls of potato salad. Sausage rolls and slices of fruit cake; hot scones; a veal and ham pie cut up into pieces. Butter in a lordly dish.

"We'll take over," Jennet whispered as she passed Martin. "Go and get something to eat."

He whistled to Blue, collected the puppy, who was handed over with the greatest reluctance, and went back to the farmhouse.

Jennet's Aunt Sarah grinned at him.

"Jennet dropped in on her way to the shop," she said. "So it was all hands to the rescue. Mike and his dad are still out searching for Tag. We cleaned out the delicatessen counter; might be a bit expensive, but it will pay in the long run. They'll be most impressed."

"How did you defrost everything?"

"I keep a store of part-baked garlic bread; only

ten minutes in the Aga and that takes about twelve loaves. Another batch just ready to come out, Dannie," she added as he erupted into the room carrying a dish of newly defrosted scones. "It's lucky that Dannie has a microwave and Aga in his cottage too."

Dannie took the garlic loaves out, broke them into pieces and piled them onto plates ready for Jennet to take across.

"Anna Wyn said not to worry about the polecat. She's feeding it and the puppy. They're doing so well she's put them on four-hourly feeds."

Which would be easier, Martin thought, and maybe they could leave out the night feed. He needed sleep. He'd never realized how exhausting it was to take on a baby animal. Yet Anna Wyn did it all the time. You took people for granted till you had to do it yourself, he thought, and patted Blue, who had come to lean against his leg.

Midge ran in asking for salt and pepper, and was there any mustard? The microwave pinged and Sarah took out another two quiches.

"Modern miracles. Good job the electricity came back or we might have had a few problems."

"The salads," Martin said, helping himself to a huge slice of quiche and potato salad. "How did you manage those?"

"The potato salad came out of pots; so did the coleslaw. I had to buy up all their stock. We grow salad stuff, remember. Didn't take long to make.

I only hope we have enough for forty. I'm not used to catering in quantity."

Everyone to the rescue. People looking for Tag. Jennet's family coming twice to help, once with the clearing up after the storm, and now with the food. People he hardly knew, who never bothered them normally but were ready to rally round as soon as there was an emergency.

"No news of Tag?" he asked, as he washed his plate under the tap, aware that everyone had to do their share.

"There was a report that he'd been seen on one of the Irish ferries with some man; but it turned out to be a father and son going back to Ireland after coming over here for a dog show. The boy was very like Tag."

"Where do they look now?" Martin asked, his voice forlorn. Where could they look? Where do you hide a pebble? On a beach. Where do you hide a boy? In a crowd of other boys. There would be boys everywhere now the summer holidays had begun. Who would notice an extra one in any group? Maybe one of his friends was hiding him. School camps and scout camps. Boys on caravan sites and tent sites.

Where was Tag's favourite place? Martin no longer knew. Tag had lost all interest in Caley, and since Dannie's engagement had not tried to tag on to him either. So who was Tag's latest hero? Perhaps Midge would know.

But Midge was busy serving lunches and answering questions.

Gwyn, in the byre, had little time to talk. Moggles' twin calves needed feeding with colostrum as they showed no intention of sucking and the cow herself was exhausted. There was little Martin could do there.

Quite suddenly he remembered that Tag had loved the Penmon woods, and often talked of camping in one of the caves. Only the caves were old mine workings and some of them were deep and many of them were treacherous. If he had gone exploring there . . .

The sun flamed from a brilliant sky, and people were flocking in. There was no time to think. The girls were busy clearing dishes away and the American visitors wanted to see round the farm.

"I can't leave Mog," Gwyn said. "You and Dannie will have to take the visitors round." He went inside the byre, carrying the equipment for the calcium drip. He'd be occupied for the rest of the afternoon.

"Don't worry," Jennet said. "Everyone is staying; my aunt and Midge . . . we can all help Anna Wyn. Off you go."

All very well but Martin had never taken a party round the farm trail before. He wished he had listened to Gwyn and knew more about the way hedges were laid and which apples they had planted in the new orchard. He knew Gwyn wanted to keep the old Welsh varieties alive.

People were sure to ask all sorts of questions. How on earth was he going to manage?

Chapter 9

Managing might have been easier if Martin's mind hadn't been filled with thoughts of Tag. Half-past two and they didn't close till five-thirty and even then there was work to be done. He had visions of Tag in the Penmon woods, trapped down a disused mine shaft.

Dannie took half of the coach load, and Martin was left with the other half: twenty people who fired questions at him all the time. He felt very young, as all were much older than his parents. He also felt very inadequate.

"What are the cows fed on?" asked one of the men.

That he could answer, as they used straw steeped in molasses, the amounts carefully worked out by top nutrition experts.

"Not made up concentrates?"

"No," Martin said. "We like to know what we're feeding and the manufacturers don't put all the ingredients onto the bags. That, they think, is how mad cow disease got into the herds. We've never had it here and sincerely hope we don't."

"Do the cows like molasses?"

"They go crazy for it. It's often used in horse feeds by trainers bringing on a horse for a top race. People have all sorts of secret recipes, but that's a common ingredient."

They had just reached the byre where the new calves were sucking from their mother. Martin put his head round the door.

"OK if they peep?" he asked.

"Just a peep. One a time."

Smiling faces came away from the door.

"Gee, I've never seen any so small as that," one lady said.

Some of the party had gone ahead and as Martin came along one of the men looked at him and said, "What in the world is this? I've never seen anything like it in my life."

"It's a paraffin heater for the incubator. We did use electricity but we keep getting power cuts here. That meant all the eggs got cold and no chicks hatched. It's up to us now; we can keep this going all day and all night if we want to."

"What are you hatching? Chickens?"

"That's the one thing we aren't hatching." Martin had to think hard. There was so much to remember, and Gwyn made it sound far more interesting than he was doing. "Since the salmonella scare, tests have to be made frequently; if they found one infected egg, we'd have to destroy the lot, and lose a fortune. They're wild bird eggs; quail, duck, geese, and ornamental birds. Some swan eggs, too; also peacocks and pheasants. Especially the fancy ones, like the Golden Pheasant, and the Lady Amherst, which is a wonderful looking bird."

He paused for breath.

"We hope to have a breeding pair next year. We don't sell our own eggs either. Just keep some for ourselves and feed the rest to animals like the pigs."

"Is salmonella a problem on your farm?"

Martin shrugged.

"It never has been. One of the vets who monitors outbreaks told me that often it's not really the eggs; it's the way they're handled. One hotel made mayonnaise from raw eggs two days before it was needed and left it in the hot kitchen; ideal for germs to breed. But the poor old eggs got the blame, not the idiots who didn't know they had set up a wonderful bug incubator."

"You sound bitter, son," somebody said.

Martin looked at him, startled. The comment made him realize how much he cared about the farming scene.

"It's made life very difficult," he said. "We had free range chickens and sold around four hundred eggs a week. Now we don't sell any. We had to cut the dairy herd in half when they dished out milk quotas. Halved our milk income. What applies to France and Germany doesn't really apply to us, only the bureaucrats in Brussels don't realize it. Their farming systems are different. Our farm would be considered large by French standards. Here it's tiny."

"So you have the Farm Trail. How else do you make money?"

"We grow barley, and oats. Sell calves for other people's milking herds. Pigs. We hoped the tea room and farm shop and the Animal Park would help, but so far they're staggering along. We've only just started them."

What else could he say? He had to give value for money and felt he was doing a rotten job.

"So many wild animals come in need of healing that much of our money goes out on vet bills and feeding them. A lot of time too," he added. "We're rearing a polecat baby and the orphaned Rottweiler, and both have had to be fed every two hours. Day and night."

"You feed them every two hours all night as well as all day?" asked a disbelieving voice.

"My sister usually does it, but I did do the polecat kitten as I found him. She does most of the work in the Sanctuary as Dannie and I have to help on the farm as well. We fit in there when we aren't tied up with the main job, which is running the farm itself. The Sanctuary is a sideline."

"And didn't start as a Sanctuary, right?" asked a voice from the back of the crowd. People got to know and started loading you with all kinds of sick animals."

Martin grinned at him. He was a big man, white haired and white bearded, with bright interested eyes.

"We started as an Animal Park, a childrens' farm, really," Martin said.

"It happens everywhere. I rescued a wild bird once and it made headlines in our local paper. Now I have a Birds' Hospital. I know, only too well, how it feels."

It was easy from then on.

"Can we see the polecat baby?" asked one of the women. Martin was relieved to discover they did want to ask questions, which meant they were interested.

"I'll show him to you -- and the pup, too -- before you go," Martin promised. He led the way to the big field where Mrs Pilkington was teaching another batch of young bullocks how to get water for themselves.

"What sort of things are wrong with the animals brought to you?" asked another of the women.

"Oiled seabirds. Gulls with botulism and other

forms of food poisoning. People throw sandwiches away that they don't want and the meat goes bad and the birds find them. They raid the litter bins and the rubbish tips. Most of them die, but Anna Wyn has saved some."

"What else?" They were crowding around him as he opened the field gate.

" A fox with a broken leg. He was run over. Pheasants get run over regularly. They're stupid birds and jay walk. Baby hedgehogs found on the road, often with a dead mother beside them. We had a young badger last year. He's gone to a sanctuary on Dartmoor."

He racked his brains for something else that was interesting.

"We've had a stray flamingo on the bird lakes in Anglesey for two years. He was brought in with a badly broken leg. He'd been too near a swans' nest and the birds attacked him. He had to be put to sleep which was sad. He was the most gorgeous pink."

Mrs Pilkington obligingly drank as they approached, fascinating everyone with the speed with which she operated the pump. She gave up her place to a young bullock who seemed to find it much more difficult, though he did manage to fill the bowl and drink.

Martin was beginning to enjoy himself. He realized he knew a lot that townspeople didn't. He had been able to answer all the questions easily, knowing the background well from listening to Gwyn and Dannie at night over supper.

His confidence grew so that when they walked back to the pig pens, he was able to tell them about the Vietnamese pot-bellied pig babies that had been born the year before, and how a local reporter had written that they were used as retrievers by shooting men to pick up game.

"Are they?" asked an astounded voice.

Martin laughed. "Not as far as we know. They wouldn't be very manageable would they?" He pointed to Charlotte, who was due to farrow soon. She walked slowly over the ground, her vast belly dragging. Alfie looked nearly as big.

"Is he the father of her babies?"

"No. He's not entire."

"Entire?" said a doubtful voice.

"We had him castrated. We didn't want him to father her babies, but we did want him as a companion for her. We took her to a boar some distance away. Don't like them bred too close, and Alfie was a rescue. We don't know his breeding."

Nobody had thought of pigs with pedigrees. Martin heard the little babble of talk with amusement.

One of the men, eager for a photograph of Ferdie operating his water tap, was leaning over the fence. Suddenly his feet slipped and he over-balanced, landing in Ferdie's swimming pool. The young pig had been playing with his tap all morning, and had a sizeable wallow underneath the pump.

There were exclamations of concern mixed with laughter as Martin leaped into the pen and helped the startled would-be photographer to his feet. Ferdie's astounded expression at the unexpected intrusion was captured on another camera, to be sent sometime later to an American local paper, where Ferdie again made headlines. "I can clean up in the coach and get my clothes changed," the man said, apparently unbothered by his adventure. He walked back to the yard.

Martin looked after him dubiously.

"There's a bathroom; he can change and wash and we all have our baggage with us," a woman said, comfortingly.

The procession moved on, crossing a narrow plank bridge that led over a stream into the apple orchard and the field with the trout pools. Martin had visions of some incautious person falling in.

"Please," he said. "Don't anyone else fall into anything. It's bad for the pigs to have people suddenly catapulting into their territory. The old Middle White boar might not be nearly so nice about it. Also there's a bull in the field next to the trout pool field. I don't recommend anyone venturing into his area. He's OK with us but we haven't tried him with people he doesn't know and I don't want to find out the hard way that he doesn't like strangers." He was relieved when his comments were greeted with laughter. He had, for some minutes, felt as if the accident were his fault.

"Don't worry, son," the courier said, as if reading his mind. "These things happen. You can't control a large group the way you can a small group and he's none the worse. Mind you, I'm glad it didn't happen to the big fellow over there. He's a pain."

Martin turned to look at an enormous noisy ginger-haired man with an immense beer belly, dressed in loud checks, who was holding forth on the way they bred pigs back home to a group of people who appeared not to be listening.

"Always get one," the courier said. Her occasionally frantic efforts reminded Martin of a shepherd he had once seen managing an extremely unruly flock without a dog to help him. "I think they might be ready for more food after this walk. How far round the farm is it?"

"About two miles from start to finish."

There was little to see in the trout pool. The apples on the orchard trees were hard and green. Everyone seemed relieved when he suggested a return to the tea room.

Dafydd the Police was waiting for him.

"No news?" Martin asked, his mood blackening. Tag had been gone for so long now.

"No. His mother says he was wearing jeans, a

112

red shirt and a blue anorak. Do you remember what he was wearing when you saw him? Could he have changed, or borrowed clothes from somewhere?"

Martin tried hard to visualize the boy.

"I was just thinking of the calf and how furious Gwyn would be if we killed it by trying to bring it out, as neither of us had ever used the calving tool before," Martin said. "It's one of our best cows too. Gwyn paid more for her than for any of the others he's bought in. I saw Tag's head pop up in the straw. We were both mad with him. It was late and we knew his parents would be worried."

"Have you any idea where he might have gone?"

Martin thought of the Penmon woods. He intended to ask Dannie to drive him there that night with Blue. But it might be a false trail; it was only a hunch.

He shook his head and felt guilty as he watched Dafydd walk away. Suppose Tag was there? The police might find him quickly; it would be another two hours before Dannie was free.

There were all the animals to feed and tidying up to do. The ponies' paddock needed cleaning up and so did the rabbit enclosure. Sighing, he fetched bucket and shovel, and walked round, the nagging worry clawing at him and growing worse minute by minute.

Chapter 10

Martin became more and more impatient as the afternoon went by. He was sure that Tag was in the Penmon woods. He would find him that evening. Tag's father would drive him there. If only the tour people would hurry. They seemed to be determined to make the visit last as long as possible. The questions were endless.

How old was the bull? Was he dangerous? How many eggs were hatched each month? Martin began to feel as if information was being dragged from him with a corkscrew, dredged up from the depths of his mind. Occasionally he had to guess and answer at random, as he had never thought about that particular subject. People asked the most astonishing questions.

At last it was five-thirty and they were able to close. The courier brought him a thick envelope.

"For the rescued animals," she said, and hurried off to the coach. Martin stared after her. The package was filled with ten pound notes. Everyone on the coach had donated and there was more than £400.

He put it in the cash box, and took that and hid it in the farm kitchen. They had a special place, in a niche behind the Aga where no one would dream of looking. The metal box was difficult to close. He wrote a note to Anna Wyn to tell her of the donation and put it on the table.

He waved to the Americans, as they crowded into their seats, and put his thumb up, as a gesture of thanks. He didn't want to delay them further, but had to acknowledge their munificence.

He looked around him as the coach drove off. His mother was back, having spent most of the day with Tag's parents. Anna Wyn, Dannie, Laura and Midge were all busy. Jennet was picking up after the ponies who invariably left unwelcome piles on the ground, usually right in everybody's way.

Surely they wouldn't miss him? If he asked, Dannie might say no.

Hastily he took the evening meal to Lola, his prize pig, now a vast matron. Caley, the pony, was out in the paddock and needed nothing to supplement his grass. Dannie would put him in his stable at dusk. The pony was never left out for twenty-four hours; too much good grass could give him laminitis.

Nobody was looking. Martin dashed into the yard, whistled to Blue, and took his bike. Only a few minutes and he'd be at Tag's home. Nobody saw him go. The dog loped beside him, keeping in to the hedge, used to this method of travelling. Martin pedalled slowly, even when cycling downhill. He had no desire to make Blue race.

The evening sun mottled the mountains, sharpening the dense crags and brightening the fields, but Martin had no eyes for that. The wind riffled his hair. Tag's voice sounded in his head, as it had done all day. I'm lost. I need you. Come and find me.

Martin knew it was his imagination but the urge was there, compelling him to try. Penmon Wood, to a boy alone, would be dark and secret and full of fear, even though there were no dragons. It was a spooky place on a fine day, a place that whispered and sang of wicked deeds, long ago. It was especially frightening when the wind howled among the trees and rain lashed the undergrowth.

Witches met by the lake in the middle of the wood, they said, and ill-wished their neighbours. The lake itself was so deep that rumour said that it went right down to Hell. No one who fell in was ever recovered. The black waters never reflected the light. It lay there, sullen and still. Martin had never seen a bird near it or a water fowl swimming over its surface.

Suppose Tag had fallen down one of the mine workings? Were there old mines in Penmon Wood? The only cave that Martin knew was shallow, reached by a long slide down. If Tag were there, he might be unable to climb out again. Especially after rain when the long slope would be slippery with mud.

There were other caves, Dannie said. Deeper, and some with several entrances. Suppose Tag had tried to explore? He was always dreaming; of finding treasure; or a cave bright with ancient paintings. Tag, always ready to speculate, was sure that there were hidden deeps on Snowdon itself where buried walls hid pictured animals that pranced and raced and pounced, and painted men with spears hunted everlastingly, unseen by any human eyes.

Tag, you idiot, Martin thought. Where are you? Why did you run away?

Nothing felt right. Tag's home, always so neat, seemed to have been hit by a whirlwind. Unwashed coffee cups littered every surface. The dining table was covered with plates, on which were half-eaten meals. Dafydd the Police was getting into his car as Martin arrived. Martin raised his eyebrows, and Dafydd shook his head.

No news.

Two nights and nearly two whole days, and no news.

Tag's mother sat, white-faced, staring at nothing. She did not notice Martin when he came to the door. Her eyes were outlined by great blue shadows, so that she looked like her own grandmother, and not the familiar happy woman that Martin knew so well.

Her husband sat on the doorstep, looking out at the hills.

"Not a sign; not a rumour, not a whisper," he said. "I thought he'd come home. I never thought he'd stay away as long as this."

"He's dead," Meg Pritchard said. "Run over, or murdered . . . " the words lay on the air.

"I think he's in Penmon Wood." Martin had to break their mood. Had to bring them back to life. Had to give them hope, although he was sure that Tag's mother had given up and was lost in an overwhelming daze of misery. "He loves the place. He's always talking about it and there are caves there. He wanted to explore them. He could easily lie up there, and camp and be quite dry. Only they might flood with the thunderstorm," he added. "And then he couldn't get out."

He wished he hadn't voiced his fears as he saw Tom's stricken face.

He might be washed out, Martin thought, and shivered, in spite of the heat.

Tom Pritchard leaped to his feet and was already on his way to the Range Rover.

"We can drive over. Coming, Meg?"

She shook her head.

"Someone needs to be here . . . he might come home, and if he couldn't get in, might go away again." Her voice was little more than a whisper and she sounded as if she didn't believe her own words.

"I'll call in and send Leah to sit with you."

"No. I'm all right. Go and look. He won't be there, but look."

"Blue could track him." Martin's mother came up the hill towards them. She was carrying a basket filled with food.

"What are you doing here?" she asked her son.

"I think Tag's in Penmon Wood. I came to tell Mr Pritchard."

"Dannie was worried about you. He didn't know where you'd gone. You didn't tell anyone. Martin, do think! We're all on edge. It's not like you to go off before the animals are fed and locked away for the night."

"Midge and Laura and Jennet were there; and I had this idea; and was in a hurry." He didn't say that he'd been afraid that Dannie wouldn't let him go. "I'm sorry. I wanted to hunt the wood before it got dark."

"Off with you. I'll stay here. I'm sure Meg

119

could do with company. Take some sandwiches; you haven't eaten enough today."

She thrust two packs into his hands and went indoors.

"Mothers!" Martin said.

"Useful people." Tag's father was impatient to be off. Martin had to run to keep up with him. Blue bounded behind them, happily unaware of any need for sorrow.

"Come on." Tom Pritchard's voice was alive again. "You'll have to direct me. I hope you know the way."

The mountains on the mainland were stark and black against the sky, the sun lighting dips and crags. On hazy days they were friendly but today they were bleak and uncompromising. Martin, sitting there, stared at them, hating them. Suppose Tag had been fool enough to go climbing? He always wanted to do what Mike did. Suppose he wasn't in Penmon Wood at all, but lying at the foot of some peak in Snowdonia?

A hunting owl flew level with the car and then dropped into the ditch.

"Anglesey owls; why don't they hunt at night like the rest of their kin?" Tom Pritchard asked, as he negotiated a steep bend and turned towards Llandonna. Anything to talk about except Tag. Just drive on, hoping against forlorn hope. Martin welcomed the change of subject.

"They seem to hunt at breakfast time and just

before dusk," he said. His mind stayed on Tag, and not on owls. Blue, lying at the rear of the car, was looking out of the window. He saw a cat and barked, the sudden noise making both of them jump. Martin quieted him.

"Tau." It was Taid's word, the Welsh for quiet. It rhymed with now and sounded like a bark. Blue put his nose on his paws and sulked.

The journey seemed to take for ever. They turned into a narrow lane bordered by a wide grass verge. Tom Pritchard parked the car just beyond a large house with a long winding drive. Two marble lions flanked the high wrought-iron gate and brooded on stone pillars.

The sun had set. Dusk shadowed the trees. A chilly wind riffled the waters of the black lake.

Martin stared at the ominous water.

He put on Blue's harness and line.

"Find Tag," he said.

The dog knew Tag. He hunted around, but showed no sign of scenting any trail.

"Where are the caves?" Tom Pritchard asked.

Martin removed the harness and let the dog run free. Blue seemed not to know why he was there. He showed no sign of co-operating and Martin felt frustrated.

"The dog can't scent him if he isn't here," Tag's father said, looking around him at the desolate trunks. He shivered.

"This is some awful place. Old Wales of the

legends. I can't think why Tag likes it."

"He likes the cave and Dannie's stories. Tales of witches and of dragons. He makes you believe they're really there. Even though I knew he was kidding, I couldn't help looking behind me every time I heard a rustle, wondering if some giant beast stood there, breathing fire. He makes the wood alive."

"Tag worships Dannie. He's his hero."

"Like Mike was, and then me, after I found him on the hill," Martin said. "Do you think he's found another hero and gone to him? Who's been around?"

They couldn't think of anyone. But then neither of them knew how Tag spent his days when he went off alone. Tag talked a lot and never told anyone anything that mattered to him.

"The kid's lonely," Tag's father said, as if he had had a sudden revelation. Martin stared at him, with a sudden vivid glimpse into all families; each member with his or her own secrets; each unable to communicate with anyone else, so that nobody knew how the others felt. What did his mother feel? Or his stepfather? What was life like seen through their eyes?

"We're all alone, really," he said. "I can't tell you how I feel. You only guess, even when I try to put it into words. You can't tell me how you feel. I guess, but I could be wrong. It's frightening."

"There are old stories of mass consciousness;

of people able to communicate by thought, of every member of the pack knowing just how every other member felt. I don't know if it's a good idea, or a bad one." Tom Pritchard's eyes never stopped searching among the trees. "Maybe I'm happier not knowing what you really think of me; and you're better off not knowing what your family think of you, or you of them."

Dusk was deepening to dark. A bat swooped down from an ivy-covered tree and Blue barked, the noise echoing and re-echoing among the trunks. "If Tag's here, he'll hear that," his father said.

"He won't know it's Blue."

The dog romped through the trees and returned to Martin, looking up at him as if asking what they expected of him. Finding no answer, he sniffed the ground, hunting his own trails.

The ground was mossy. They walked silently along the narrow trail. Not a sign of life other than birdlife. Not a footprint in the mud. No answer to their echoing calls.

Overhead long clouds streamed across the darkening sky. Martin knew as well as any weather forecaster what the sky foretold. It was another skill that Taid had taught him and he had never known till now that it was a skill.

A gale is due, those streamers said.

The wind whispered in the trees. The whispers grew to a rustle. The rustle grew to an ominous roar. Blue walked at Martin's heels, so close that he brushed his leg. The dog's eyes were anxious. He hated wind, especially when it came from behind and blew through his fur.

The trail led through the tiny wood. They found four caves. Each was deserted. Dead leaves blew in the wind. Up the scree and down the peaty side, searching vainly, until they both had to admit that nobody could be hidden there. Blue showed no sign of interest in anything but the smells of wild animals on the ground.

Suddenly the dog's head went up and his eyes glinted with interest.

"Listen." Martin grabbed Tom Pritchard's sleeve, stopping him in mid stride.

There was a whimpering on the wind, a forlorn crying. A child sobbing? A frightened boy on his own?

Blue bounded off, his tail waving. A few minutes later they heard him bark. Tom and Martin crashed through the bushes, homing in on the dog.

"Tag!" Tom's voice was excited.

Martin had already seen why the dog was barking. A tiny puppy was tied fast to one of the trees. It whined and pulled at the choking rope in its efforts to get free, half-strangling itself. Blue licked its head.

Tom Pritchard took a penknife from his pocket and cut the rope. He lifted the pup, which licked his sombre face.

"Tag isn't here," he said. "He'd never have left a dog tied up like that. He'd have done something to try and get it free. If he were here, he'd have heard it crying."

Martin took the puppy from him. Another mouth to feed. Another row with Gwyn. Hatred for the human race swept over him, despairingly. Silently, they walked back through the shadowed trees, each lost in his own disappointment. Blue followed, occasionally trying to lick at the pup.

Back at the Range Rover Martin gave the puppy water to drink. It lapped as if it had been thirsty for days.

Martin looked down at their find. The little dog needed a bath. Its white coat was filthy. It had a black patch over one eye, that gave it a jaunty appearance. Some Jack Russell. Some collie, maybe, and a lot of goodness knows what. It licked his hand and stared up at him, its eyes anxious. He was so angry it hurt.

"Patch," Martin thought. No other name would suit. As the small body shifted against his hand he knew that he now had another dog, and this little one was going to stay, even if he had to fight for the right to keep it.

I was meant to go to Penmon Wood today, he thought. Even if Tag wasn't there. We've saved the pup's life. I wonder who tied him up and left him alone, terrified, at the mercy of any fox that came by. Even if it weren't killed by a predator, it would have died of hunger. Anger and misery made Martin feel sick. It couldn't be more than a few months old. Even as he looked at it, the pup licked trustingly at the hand that held him. It sighed deeply and burrowed into the warm shirt, seeking contact and comfort.

The side of its body felt rough, and Martin, looking at the fur, gave a deep infuriated grunt.

"Something wrong?" asked Tom Pritchard.

"He's been burned; there's a round burn as if someone stubbed out a cigar on him. People who do things like that should have it done to them!"

Martin could have attacked the person who had injured the dog. He had a sudden memory of Anna Wyn's yell when she found the abandoned kittens.

"I hate people."

For the first time he understood exactly how his stepsister felt.

The lanes were endless, one turning aftern another. The journey back seemed longer than that out. There was no hope now to buoy them.

They were more than halfway home when Tom Pritchard spoke again. He had been lost in his own despair.

"How will we tell them? They're expecting us to have Tag."

Martin didn't know.

Chapter 11

Martin had forgotten how to sleep. Outside the wind whistled, and a fox barked, far away. A distant train rattled towards Holyhead. A car started in the lane and sped into the darkness, headlights raking his ceiling.

He sat up, wondering if he would ever sleep again. He thumped his pillow and turned it over. He lay on his back, stretching out, wishing he could forget the world, but still sleep wouldn't come.

Tag was out there, somewhere in the darkness. Tag alone. Tag dead? Thoughts of all kinds of horrors refused to be stilled. He tried counting, but Tag came back into his mind.

Two whole days and this was the third endless

night. Not a sign, not a hint, not a sighting that was genuine. People had rung in from all over the country when his face appeared on TV. A boy had been seen in Edinburgh who looked like Tag. He had been reported from Brighton and from Abergavenny. From Cardiff and at Heathrow. None of the boys was Tag.

Martin thought wearily of the policemen searching the moors, of the mountain rescue people out on the hills, of every household hunting through shed and outhouse, and farmers searching the barns. Stores and warehouses and disused buildings. Not a trace, not a clue, not a glimmer of hope.

Martin thumped his pillow again. Why should he care about Tag who was such a nuisance, Tag with his constant noise and constant questions; and his constant disobedience.

Tag laughing, Tag playing with Blue, Tag bringing a badly made birthday present, eager for praise. Tag's mother, who most certainly would not be asleep, his father who was hunting through wood and gully, driving endlessly, his eyes dark and shadowed with fear.

Midge, who never seemed to care, sobbing in a corner of the stable, her face buried in Caley's mane. Martin, going to feed the pony, had crept away, knowing she wouldn't want to be seen.

Even Jennet, who was always so serene, had snapped at everyone that afternoon. Her bright chatter was silenced, and she worked, as they all did, without exchanging a word.

Jennet. Martin thought of her, longing to ask her out for a date, yet always afraid, sure she would laugh and toss her head and go her own way. She seemed to have little time for him. Yet, when she was there, he was aware of no one else, and that annoyed him. He saw her face in his dreams and saw it now, in his mind's eye, her soft hair and quiet contained face, her unawareness of him, all the time.

It was nearly as bad to think of Jennet as to think of Tag.

If only they hadn't sent him home.

Martin got out of bed and stood at the window, looking at the bright half moon that shone on the distant hills. Moonlight patterned the ground. A fox ran swiftly across the cobbles and vanished into the distance, fleetfoot up the wall and over the grass.

Light from Dannie's cottage flashed across the yard.

Martin dragged on jeans and shirt and jersey, laced his shoes, and ran softly downstairs, whistling to Blue as he went. The dog sprang from his bed, tail waving, delighted to have action in the middle of the night. He missed the pup, who Dai had taken that day. The new rescue watched them. He seemed to have settled in.

Martin knocked on Dannie's door.

"1 a.m. and all is far from well," Dannie said, as he opened it. " Cant you sleep either? Coffee? I'm going hunting. Want to come?"

"I cant think of anything but Tag," Martin said. "Anything to be doing, not just thinking. If we hadn't sent him home . . . "

"If all the world were paper, and all the sea were ink." There was irritation in Dannie's voice.

"What's that supposed to mean?"

"It's an old rhyme. Haven't heard it for years and I cant remember it properly. Jennet came out with it yesterday. I think it goes on if all the trees were bread and cheese what would we have to drink?"

It was the sort of silly rhyme that Tag would love. He was always telling absurd riddles, about elephants in cherry trees and why did the chicken cross the road. Retarded development, Midge said.

Dannie irritable was as bad as Tag lost.

"So where are we looking?" Martin asked.

"Parys Mountain."

"Why would he go there?"

"Midge said he's been reading about the old mine workings. His father had a book about them. He's writing about Welsh legends, remember?"

"Are there any legends about the mines?"

"Bound to be. Wales is well haunted. There's even supposed to be a singing woman at Wylfa, down in the deeps below the power station. The workmen heard her when they were building the place. You cant get much more modern than that. And the mines are old . . . very old workings, back in history. Anyway Tag was talking about finding gold nuggets."

"Is there a gold mine there?"

"No idea. But there are mines and kids have been lost in them before now; and some of the workings are deep. And Tag is nuts. Remember how he tried to climb the cliffs at South Stack and got stuck and Mike had to rescue him. Lucky he didnt have the whole works out that day. "

"He got marooned on a sandbank and one of the yachtsmen had to rescue him. " Martin had forgotten about both incidents. Tag had been eight years old when he was marooned and nearly ten when he tried to climb the cliffs at South Stack.

Remembering didn't help. It made matters far worse, What sort of lunacy had Tag been up to now?

"Doesn't bear thinking about," Dannie said.

They drank the scalding coffee fast.

"Come on," Dannie grabbed his anorak. "He's probably panning for gold, or trying to find his way through an old mine working . . . "

"Or hitchhiked to Manchester and stowed away on a plane to visit his grandmother." Martin's voice was morose. Tag was capable of anything.

"Let's be off. Need handlamps and plenty of light. The moon'll be hidden by cloud soon. Only hope it doesn't rain. The storm didn't clear the air. There's still thunder about."

The lanes were empty, the headlights slashing the dark. Dannie drove fast, along the A4080, through Newborough and Maltreath, both dark and silent, everyone sleeping. Past the dunes at Aberffraw, ghostly in the moonlight, and Cable Bay where an irritable sea pounded against the rocks. The headlights glittered on the spume.

They had a clear road to the Rhos Neigr crossroads, and then they were on the A5. Several freightliners passed them, travelling fast through the night. One car overtook them, and then they were on their own, at journey's end. The little mountain reared against the darkening sky, hiding secrets.

Martin put Blue's harness on. Without much hope, but to his surprise the dog pulled strongly over to a large furze clump. Dannie peered inside.

"The little coot's bike. And it hasn't been here long. It's quite dry and it rained last night."

"It would have dried by now."

"This wouldn't. It'd be soaked."

It was the psychedelic haversack that Midge had given Tag for his birthday. Fluorescent green and red and purple gleamed in the light of the handlamp. Dannie opened it to find a spare jersey, a pair of dirty socks, and three bars of chocolate.

"He apparently wasn't starving. Or he'd have eaten these or taken them with him."

Martin was concentrating on his dog.

"Find Tag." Blue looked at him, as if considering, and then began to search the ground.

The path was pitted and bumpy. Grey rocks threatened to trip them. Heather clumps teased them. Trailing brambles snatched at legs. The moon was a faint memory, caught in cloud.

Blue nosed on, and on, climbing steadily. Over a little hummock, and then paused by a gaping hole. He barked. Faint as a breath came a small cry from below.

"Help. I cant get out."

Dannie, lying flat, shone the hand lamp down the hole.

"Tag. It's Martin and Dannie. Can you see us? Are you hurt?"

Tag gave a little wail, and a half sob of relief.

"No. I climbed down. It was easy to the ledge but then the wall gave way and sort of avalanched. It's slippery and I cant find a way back. I fell much further than I meant to. I can just see your light. I'm in a sort of cave thing. The earth that fell is banked up and so slippery I cant climb over it. I just fall back all the time." There was a catch in his breath. "It's so dark and I'm cold."

Martin was ridiculously reminded of Alice

133

falling down the rabbit hole. Tag was safe and if he could have put his hands on him he would have punched him in relief and fury. Stupid little nut. Now what did they do?

"This time it's all stations out to rescue him," Dannie said. "Can you and Blue stay here and keep him company? Whatever you do dont try to reach him or there'll be two of you in trouble. You could get hurt, or land up dead, and that wouldn't help Tag."

Dannie's voice was anxious as if he were sure that once he had gone Martin would try some idiotic rescue ploy and climb down into the pit.

"I wont do anything, I promise."

"See you dont, even if he sounds desperate. I'll drive to a call box and phone the police. Tell them the kid's safe and we need . . . who in heaven's name do we need? Search and Rescue? Fire Brigade? The Underwater Team?" Relief had gone to Dannie's head. His words spilled over themselves.

"Police anyway." Dannie was talking so fast he hadn't time to breathe. "Ambulance probably . . . he ought to be checked in hospital. And they must tell his parents; that's vital. See you." He sounded almost light hearted. But a lot could still go wrong. Suppose more of the shaft gave way and Tag was smothered by mud?

Martin, listening to his friend's receding foot-steps, felt he had lost all comfort. He had never before thought of Dannie as a friend. He looked at that idea in amazement and knew it to be true. Dannie was the best friend he had ever had.

Rain, previously threatening on the strengthening wind, became a reality. Could the shaft flood? Hurry, Dannie, hurry. Martin visualised all kinds of accidents, all of them ending in Tag's death. He lay, trying to see down, holding on to Blue for comfort.

"Martin?"

The small voice sounded scared. "I'm here." There was nothing like yelling down a deep hole in the ground to someone you couldn't even see.

"I'm hungry. Can you throw my chocolate down? I had some sandwiches but I ate those ages ago. Did you find my bike?"

"Blue found it. I can try to chuck some down but I bet it wont reach you."

"I've got a torch. The battery's nearly dead, but it's still OK for a bit."

Martin had to remember where the bike was hidden; had to find the haversack, which they had left there. Had to take the chocolate bars and climb back again to the pitshaft. It looked darker than before.

There was a faint glim far below him. The hole was much deeper than he had thought. The sides near the top were rough and climbable, but then the earth slid away and left a steep slippery gash that had no footholds at all.

Martin crouched at the gaping mouth. There had been barricades around it, but they were fallen and broken and some had been stolen for firewood. Few people ever came to this desolate place. Civilisation was a memory, although there were homes and farms not too far away.

The dark isolated them. The road below was only there when a rare car or lorry pounded its way along, headlights flooding the sky.

"I'll throw one bar down at a time," Martin said, out of breath with hurrying. "Yell if you find it. I wont let you have the others for half an hour or so."

He shone his torch and hurled the chocolate, throwing it out from him so that, hopefully, it wouldn't lodge halfway down and be unreachable. Endless minutes passed. He thought he saw a faint gleam far below, and then it died.

"Got it." There was satisfaction in Tag's voice. "How did you find me? Dont go away."

"Dannie's gone for help. I wont go, I promise. It was something Midge said. How long have you been there?"

"Not that long; since about dinner time today. I had money with me and bought fish and chips at lunchtime. I went to Penmon Wood first. I slept in the Dragon Cave. It's smelly. I pinched some of Dannie's goose eggs; they were a bit stale, but I cooked them over a bonfire. I had matches."

Dannie and his daft stories, Martin thought. Aloud, he said,

"I hope you didn't set the wood alight."

"I did it all properly," Tag was indignant, his voice only just audible. "It's too creepy there. Noises in the trees and strange bird sounds and I felt there were spooks around." He stopped talking for what seemed an age. Then the thin voice came again, muffled, and broken as if perhaps he were crying.

"I was scared to go home after I'd been away so long. I hid in barns and sheds, but never for long, in case someone found me. "He laughed shakily. "I was in your barn during the thunderstorm. I had to get out through gaps in the wall when the tree came down. Nobody I met ever looked at me twice. I wish they had."

For the first time he sounded as if he realised what he had done.

"Everyone's been hunting for you, you little ass." Martin's voice was rough with anger, as he thought of the desperate days and the fears that had been growing for the child's safety. "Your mother's sure you're dead. Your father hasn't been to bed since you disappeared. Tag, are you listening?"

"Yes, " said the small voice. " I didn't think they'd care. They're always cross with me. So are you and Dannie. " There was a brief silence, during which Martin felt a stab of guilt, then the little voice spoke again. "I'm tired. I'm going to sleep, now I'm safe. Dont go, will you? Where's Dannie? Why did he go?" He seemed to have forgotten he had already asked.

"Gone for help, you coot. I told you. We cant get you out. It's going to need a massive effort and all the experts. They'll hate your guts."

"They'll all be heroes and on the telly. They wont hate me at all. They'll be doing what they're trained for."

Martin had forgotten Tag's peculiar logic, and his blithe certainty that the whole world existed to help him out of his various scrapes. Did he ever appreciate the danger, Martin wondered.

He lay in the rain, wishing he had put on a waterproof jacket. The moon had long vanished and the clouds were full and emptying solidly. He was cold and soaked, all because of Tag. Dannie had been gone for ever. Suppose he had an accident on the way to phone? Maybe the phones were all out of order. He couldn't knock anyone up. Not in the middle of the night. Or would he, if he were desperate?

Martin shone the torch on his watchface. Four a.m. Soon be milking time and Gwyn wouldn't be pleased to find both of them missing. It was cold on the hillside. Suppose the old ghosts walked?

It was long past midnight though, so he ought to be safe. Did ghosts harm you?

It was easy to believe, lying there alone in

the dark and the rain, except for his dog and a small boy trapped far beneath him, that spirits had power to hurt. Martin shivered.

He tried to remember being twelve and whether he had got into such scrapes as Tag. He was sure he hadn't. He was much more fearful than Tag, imagining disasters that rarely happened. If only the rain would ease. It was sheeting from the sky and above the hissing sound of its fall came an ominous rumble from the distant hills. Lightning forked across the mountains. The brief hot weather always seemed to end in storms. Blue hid his face under Martin's jacket, ignoring the soaked cloth.

"Tag?" There was no sound. Unbelievably, Tag must have fallen asleep. He couldn't be dead in that time, could he?

The wind nudged Martin's hair, Blue crept against him, not liking the darkness and the strange scents on the air. Martin crouched against a rock.

There, sitting in the darkness and the wet, he came to a surprising decision. He felt Taid beside him, offering advice and hope.

He would go to agricultural college, and not become a vet. He would study finance, and make the farm the most profitable in Anglesey. He felt a sudden affection for his step family. If Tag was safely rescued . . . he made promises to Fortune.

And then realised that even if the rescue went awry, as well it might, he owed his family. They cared for him, maybe more than he cared for Tag, who was so much younger, and not ever really a friend.

People mattered.

He knew now how his mother felt; he appreciated his stepfather's worries; he could guess at the girls' feelings and their problems and he shared Dannie's. Though falling in love was something he didn't understand.

Or did he?

Jennet's face swam in front of his eyes and he knew that if it were she who was lost down the mine he would try to reach her, even if it meant his death. Was that love? What was love? The romantic nonsense in the magazines that his stepsisters read, or something different, a deep caring about other people, and maybe about one person in particular. Or a whole family.

Jennet. If only he could get to know her better, If only she would look at him as if she saw him.

He couldn't talk to her and seldom had anything to do with her, never knowing how to answer her chatter. She was always busy now in the sanctuary when she was not taking children pony trekking. She seemed to care for animals more than she did for people. He put his arms around his dog, and stared into a future that opened out surprisingly in front of him, offering all sorts of hidden goals and devious pathways.

There were ghosts on the hill. He heard rustles and once a piercing whistle as if some man was working a dog. There was a clatter of running hooves, and four sheep passed him, as if driven.

They vanished. Far below he heard the welcome sound of voices, and saw headlights and the blue flashing lights of the police cars.

"Tag," he called down the hole.

There was no answer. Martin sat, hugging his knees, his teeth chattering uncontrollably. He wondered if perhaps they had been deluded and heard voices when there were none. Or perhaps Tag was there, and had died of fear and cold. If only he could see to the bottom of the hole.

He listened to the pounding feet that ran up the path. Hope was a memory, and despair governed him. He was sure the rescuers had come too late.

Chapter 12

Lightning ripped the sky. Thunder boomed and the steady rain drummed down, bouncing on the rock. There were men coming up the hill. Torches shone, and in the intermittent silences voices spoke.

Rain, seeping into the ground. Rain, driving into the pit opening. Rain, flooding the tunnels. Rain, making the steep slippery slope even more slippery. How would they get Tag out? With ropes, with climbers, who slid down into the depths, and were hauled back again?

"Martin!"

Tag's voice startled him.

"I'm scared. There's water . . . "

"It'll be OK. People are coming up the hill

now," Martin said, not sure at all that it would be OK. Not sure at all that they would bring Tag up alive. How much water? Where was it coming from? He dared not ask.

He stared, dazzled, into the eye of a torch. Blue growled, deep in his throat, sure they were threatened.

Martin quieted the dog.

"Sorry, son. Didn't mean to blind you. Down there, is he? Still talking?"

"He says there's water . . . "

"There'll be more, with this lot coming down and no sign of easing. " The hillside seemed alive with hurrying men and calling voices.

Dannie was beside him.

"We're ordered back to the farm for milking. And you need to get out of those wet clothes or you'll be joining Tag in hospital."

"I want to stay."

"Sorry, son." The big policeman's voice was brusque, and unfamiliar with its Lancashire accent. Martin hadn't realised how used he was to the soft Welsh lilt. Even Dannie had a trace of it. "There's nothing you can do. You're soaked to the skin, and it'll be hours before we get him up. First we'll let someone down on a rope to be with him."

"Cant I go? He knows me."

"He'll soon know all of us. Be off, now. We dont want any more casualties. You'd both be in the way."

The ambulance, just pulling up at the end of the path, was an ominous sign. One of the attendants, jumping out, looked at Martin.

"Hey, off with those clothes and into the blankets," he said.

"I'm not going to hospital."

"No need. You can return the blankets tomorrow. Put the Land Rover heater full on and get him warm," he added to Dannie.

"Blue had better sit under the heater, at your feet. He's as wet as you are. Damn this rain." Dannie was wet too but he at least had had the sense to wear a waterproof jacket.

Martin changed in the ambulance and dived into the Land Rover, rain drumming on the road. He hugged the blankets round him. They scratched his skin. Blue jumped in after him and sat huddled at his feet. Glancing back, Martin saw lights bobbing above him. Cars were parked along the road.

The warmth and movement lulled him. The constant whine of the windscreen wipers was a background to the storm. Lightning zigged and zigged again and the lower peaks were outlined briefly against the sky. The high peaks were hidden.

It wasn't over yet. Tag was found but far from safe and the longer the rain continued the more danger of flooding in the workings. It would have been better to stay, to know what was happening.

Or would it?

"It's worse for his parents," Dannie said. "They were told to sit and wait for news. His father wanted to come."

Waiting . . . that was far worse than being involved. Tag would know if he were safe or not. Those who were at home would have hours to spend before they heard any news, good or bad.

Dannie drove in to the farmyard.

Gwyn, grimfaced, just up for milking, met them, his eyes angry.

"Where on earth have you been? You didn't ask if you could have the Land Rover."

" You were asleep." Dannie brushed his wet hair out of his eyes. "Midge said Tag was interested in Parys Mountain. We couldn't sleep and went to look. He's fallen down one of the old mine shafts. They're getting him up now."

I hope, Martin thought, his fingers crossed. Gwyn stared at him.

"Funny way to dress."

"He got soaked, sitting by the mineshaft to keep Tag company."

"Better get to bed." Gwyn strode off to fetch the cows.

Martin dragged himself upstairs. His mother took one look at him and ran a warm bath. The water, and a mug of sweet coffee, revived him. He dressed, and went down to take his place

145

in the milking parlour. He couldn't sleep and couldn't stay in bed. He needed to be doing.

The day took its normal course, though nothing felt normal. The empty cage used for emergencies in the animal sanctuary was covered, a rustle coming from inside. He took off the curtain that kept out the light and stared down into the amber eyes of a half grown fox cub. "Someone found him lying by the road yesterday," Anna Wynn said. "He's been worried by dogs; probably terriers. Several bites and a very badly damaged leg."

"He seems half tame." The cub was sitting, head on one side, watching them. He pawed at the mesh with his uninjured leg.

"I think he's quite tame. He's either been kept deliberately as bait, or someone has had him since he was tiny and then let him go. He's not nearly wary enough."

She put down a plate of dog meal, and the little animal tucked himself up neatly, like a small cat, and began to eat, oblivious to everything else.

Martin's thoughts were not on his work. They were on Parys Mountain, wondering what was happening. He brushed Caley, his mind far away, and was rewarded for his inattention by a sudden sharp nip on his arm.

The pigs grunted to him and were dismayed when he left without a glance back. Laura and Midge joined them at nine o' clock, but nobody felt like talking. They worked in silence, cleaning pens and fetching food and water.

"How's your mum?" Martin asked Midge.

"Desperate. There's still no news. It's been hours. That policeman called, in the middle of the night, to say Tag was found, but they'd be sometime yet before he was safe." At least the rain had stopped. The morning was dull, with a promise of sun later, and rifts in the clouds to show blue sky. The cooler weather livened the animals.

Cleo, the shaggy black lamb, was frisking in her paddock. The rabbits played chase me Charlie in their enclosure. Martin checked for new burrows, and filled the holes with rocks. Soon it would be all rock, he thought, as he discovered that a young black rabbit had almost tunnelled out.

He went back to the kitchen for a drink, and Blue greeted him, his new charge curled up on the big dog's bed. Gwyn, in for his morning break, looked at his stepson.

"Caught it from your sisters," he said.

"Caught what?"

"This passion for rescuing everything that comes begging."

"Can Patch stay?"

"Everyone else seems to think he can. Who am I to go against all of you?" Gwyn gave him a sudden grin. "OK, son. I'd not have any of you different. We'll all be feeling better when the little lad's home safe."

At lunchtime someone switched on the news. News of Tag. Men were working to bring him to the surface, but the rains had made it very difficult. He had a companion now and they had lowered food for him, but the water was seeping into the tunnel where he was trapped and still rising.

The camera showed a wall of mud that blocked the way into the main working where Tag was waiting, knee deep in water. The man who had been lowered down the shaft was digging it away, but had to be careful. There was little room to move. The pit was narrow.

Nobody felt better for seeing the difficulties.

"They have to make the most of it. It's probably mostly not true," Dannie said, never believing anything that was written in the newspapers, and positive that cameras could lie too.

Martin, unable to concentrate, went to help Jennet in the shop, but after giving the wrong change several times, she sent him out again.

"She doesn't seem in the least worried," he complained to Dannie.

"Our Jennet's doesn't show it," Dannie said. "It doesn't mean she doesn't feel it. She maybe feels it worse."

Martin wanted to go to her, to offer comfort, though he had no idea how. One of the visitors asked him about the young fox, and then Laura called him to carry tea trays to people sitting at the picnic benches. He was soon too busy to even remember Tag, except for brief flashes of worry.

By five o'clock the last of the visitors had gone.

"They must have him out by now." Martin was feeling sick. Something had gone wrong. Tag was drowned and nobody wanted to tell them.

His mother came flying out of the farmhouse and yelled across the yard.

"Tag's safe. On his way to hospital for a check up but he's in pretty good shape, they said."

The sun overhead was brighter, the air warmer, the chores less demanding. Dannie began to whistle. Midge flew to her bicycle and was off home almost before they had time to say anything at all. Anna Wyn hugged Laura, tears spilling down both their faces.

Jennet laughed, and suddenly hugged Martin, who felt as if the world had begun to whirl.

"He's safe, he's safe, he's safe," she said, speaking for all of them.

They all piled in to watch the news; to see the men on the mountainside, busy with their equipment, to see Tag hauled to the surface, filthy, but grinning, raising one thumb to the camera.

They saw him on the stretcher, loaded into the

ambulance, and heard his father say briefly that they were overjoyed, before shepherding his wife through the hospital doors.

Martin slept that night as if he had never slept before and woke reluctantly to face the day. There seemed more work than ever, as he swept and cleaned up and carried water. Blue and the Patch had to be fed. The polecat and the Rotti pup were now in one of the empty aviaries. The little polecat came to greet him, tail sweeping the ground, and the bright eyed head seemed to smile at him.

The pup rolled over for its tummy to be rubbed.

"I'm not sure if the polecat thinks he's a puppy or the pup thinks he's a polecat," Jennet said, her voice amused. "I'm sure they're both mixed up."

The day was brighter.

When he went to the fox cage, a small figure was crouched over it.

"Tag! I thought you were in hospital."

Tag's irrepressible grin brightened his face.

"They cant keep a good man down," he said. "Dad's coming later to thank you. He says if it wasn't for you I'd have been killed long ago; sort of guardian angel."

"I dont feel like one. And dont you ever do anything like that again. Time your grew up, you limb of Satan."

There was a basket at Tag's feet.

"That's why I climbed down," he said. Three tiny fluffy black kittens stared up at Martin. "I saw some man chuck them down into the shaft. They were alive, so I went after them. I didn't think I'd fall. Mum says I can keep one and Anna Wyn can have the other two."

"We'll need to find homes for the other two," Martin said. "How did you keep them alive?" "I tucked them under my jersey. They were warmer than I was. They weren't hurt. They slid down."

Martin looked at him, exasperated.

"You do the daftest things. Let's take the kits to Anna Wyn. They need feeding."

"Mum fed them. They've had some bread and milk."

"I thought they'd keep you in hospital," Martin said, after they'd delivered the kittens to Anna Wyn.

"They did, for the night. I asked dad to come for me real early. I was OK. But gee, was I scared! Only I knew it would be all right when you and Dannie came." They had gone back with food for the fox. Tag held out a finger to the cub, who promptly bit it.

"Serve you right, " Martin said. "You dont learn, do you? Come on. Let's get that dressed."

"I'm full of anti tet, so that's OK. Why did he bite me? I didn't want to hurt him."

"How's he supposed to know that? You poke a

finger at him. Nobody else has been daft enough to do that."

Tag would never change, Martin thought, exasperated, as he bathed the bite and covered it with plaster. Some people never learn.

"Best go home. You dont want search parties out for you all over again," he said, as Tag walked to the kitchen door. For once, he was obeyed without question.

"They knew I was bringing the kittens, " he said, as he rode off.

Everyone seemed to be bubbling with high spirits.

His mother behaved as if she were hugging some secret and spent most of the day talking on the phone. Dilys and Tony were home early, and came to help with the animals.

Martin whistled to both his dogs and took them off for a riot in the empty paddock, where neither could come to harm. Blue chased the pup as if he too were only a few months old. The sun dappled the meadow and swallows flew among the trees. Blue, suddenly exultant, chased their flying shadows on the grass, the pup trying his best to keep up.

There was no meal ready in the kitchen at suppertime. Martin, looking at the table with disbelief, thought he had never been so hungry in his life, and where was the food?

The knock on the door startled him.

"Good of your Mam to ask me, " Dai the Police said, unfamiliar in grey gaberdine trousers and a smart suede jacket, his blonde head bare.

Martin felt as if he had stepped into a soap opera and nobody had told him the lines. There was a burst of laughter from the rarely used dining room.

Anna Wyn, coming into the kitchen too fast, almost bumped into Dai.

"Come on, both of you. We're waiting for you," she said.

The room was packed. Tag and Midge and their parents. Dilys and Tony, Jennet, laughing at him. Dannie with his arm round Ann Wyn. Laura and Mike, and their parents, all of them laughing and excited, thankful that Tag's adventure had ended well.

"We thought we'd celebrate," Leah said, looking at her son. "Martin, have you forgotten what day it is?"

He stared at the table, piled high with parcels, at the birthday cake, which said Happy Birthday, Martin. Today he was eighteen. He had completely forgotten.

"We thought we wouldn't plan the celebration till we were sure Tag was safe," Leah said. "He managed to come home just in time, so we can have a double celebration."

Martin was sudeny aware of excitement exploding inside him, of a desire to hug everyone, to shout and to dance. Only his glinting eyes revealed his feelings. Today he had his own small income, left to him in trust by Taid. Today he had to decide his future. But he had already decided, there on the hill in the dark, waiting for Tag's rescuers.

Happy birthday to you, they sang, and raised their glasses to him. He was part of the family, belonging. And yet not belonging. Everyone had a partner, except him. Tag had his family. His mother had Gwyn and Anna Wyn had Dannie who would have less time for Martin when they were married. Dilys and Tony . . . and Jennet. Jennet. Jennet.

He looked across the room and saw he watching him. She lifted her thumb, her eyes saying be happy. Martin, and for a moment he forgot everything and plunged into dreams.

Then he pulled himself back to the present, to listen to the excited voices around him and feel his own excitement mounting with the future in front of him, and his courage building so that tonight he would ask Jennet to come out with him.

"Our thanks for finding Tag."

Tom Pritchard handed a large parcel to Dannie and another to Martin. Both were remarkably heavy.

"Weddings and a birthday . . . couldn't be better," he said.

Dannie was staring at a canteen of cutlery.

Martin looked at the little portable television set.

"We didn't do much, but thanks," he said, feeling the words inadequate.

"If you hadn't found him then, he would have been drowned. They got him out just in time." Tom Pritchard squeezed his son's shoulder. "He deserves a good thrashing for being so daft."

"What are you going to do with grandfather's money?" Leah asked, aware of a sudden pain in Tag's eyes. It was a moment before Martin realised she meant Taid. "Go to Agricultural College. It takes too long to be a vet and besides, we'll have Tony." He grinned at his stepbrother-to-be. "Then I'll show you how to run the farm properly," he added, turning to Gwyn.

"That'll be the day. Us old ones do know some things, son." Gwyn began to carve the joint. Leah passed the plates.

Martin, loading his with roast potatoes and peas and carrots and Yorkshire pudding, wondered where he would be this time next year. The girls would be married. He looked at Jennet, who seemed lost in her own dreams. Was he perhaps a part of them?

Once he had thought that growing up would be easy. Now he knew that growing up often hurt.

Tag, spiking a potato on his fork, eating the way they did in America, held up his trophy and winked at Martin. Who felt a sudden enormous envy because at twelve he had been bitter and angry and life had been hateful, and never could he face the world with spirits as light as Tag's.

Gwyn, catching his stepson's glance, read the thought.

"To Martin," he said. "Who has made more difference to us all than he will ever realise."

"The stuff that heroes are made of," Dai the Police said, grinning, and the echoes of the past came on the air from Taid. "Only those who feel fear are real heroes. The others are too stupid."

Late that night, when the moon was high, Martin took the dogs for their last run. Quite suddenly, as he watched them frolic, he felt as mad as they and raced with them through the darkness until he was breathless. He left the field by vaulting the gate. Blue leaped after him and the Jackie crawled under.

He wanted to yell his pleasure and excitement at the sky, but the farmhouse and the cottage were dark. Everyone was sleeping. He leaned on the gate and looked into the shadowy sanctuary. An owl hooted from a distant tree.

Maybe the world wasn't such a bad place. All his life lay ahead. Perhaps in the future there would be a home for him and Jennet. Anna Wynn and Dilys would have children. Nothing stayed the same, ever.

"Brooding about life?" Gwyn asked from the darkness. Martin jumped. He had thought that everyone was in bed, and hadn't heard his step-father approach. The dogs lay at his feet, panting. They never barked at Gwyn.

"Thinking about Taid and his "if onlys"," Martin said. "He always said they were a waste of time."

"Like what?"

"If my mother hadn't been ill . . . hadn't come to Wales . . . hadn't married you . . . I'd never have been standing here, knowing it was the place I love best on earth," Martin said. The words hadn't been in his mind. They'd sprung from him, startling him almost as much as they startled and pleased his stepfather.

"I think maybe it's all for the best, though at times no one would ever have thought so." Gwyn clapped his stepson on the shoulder. " Bed, or we'll never be up for milking."

Martin stood at his bedroom window looking out, wishing he hadn't to leave, even for short while. Three years was a long time and he'd only spend part of it here. And then he'd be home for good.

Home. It was a wonderful word. He was eighteen years old and an exciting life lay ahead. Blue nosed his knee. He'd miss his dogs. Nothing was ever simple; there were always shadows in the sunshine.

Maybe living was just learning to cope, and make the best of whatever happened to you.

He wished he'd known that six years ago. He wondered if Tag would ever learn it. He heard the memoried echo of Taid's voice again, just before he fell asleep.

" One day you'll be old, like me, and life slipping away from you. Make the most of what you have, boy. You never get a second chance."